We Make Mud

DZANC BOOKS

1334 Woodbourne Street
Westland, MI 48186
www.dzancbooks.org

Some of what's inside this book first appeared on the insides of these other
publications: *Agriculture Reader, Alaska Quarterly Review, Another Chicago
Magazine, Best of the Web 2009, Bombay Gin, Brass Sopaipilla, Caketrain,
Chicago Review, Denver Quarterly, Detroit: Imaginary Cities, Detroit Noir,
Dislocate, Double Room, Drunken Boat, elimae, Eyeshot, failbetter, Fiddleback,
Flyway, Hobart, Listen Up, LitRag, MadHatter's Review, Midwest Quarterly,
Necessary Fiction, New York Tyrant, Phoebe, Post Road, Powell's North Reading
Series Broadside, PP/FF: An Anthology, Saltgrass, Salt Hill, Sleeping Fish, Snow
Monkey, Stickman Review, Taint, Tarpaulin Sky, Third Coast, Typo, Unsaid,
Verse, Word Riot,* and *Willow Springs.*

Ten of these stories also appeared in the chapbook
The Moon is a Fish published by Cinematheque Press.

Published 2011 by Dzanc Books
Book design by Steven Seighman
Cover art by Astrid Cravens

06 07 08 09 10 11 5 4 3 2 1
First edition July 2011
ISBN-13: 978-0982631836

Printed in the United States of America

WE
MAKE
MUD

stories

PETER
MARKUS

DZANC
BOOKS

WHAT'S INSIDE
THIS BOOK

This book is for

Helena
who put the word *brother* under my tongue

for Sol
the word *brother* made flesh

and for Beck
for making all this mud possible.

And in memory of

Bob

The Singing Fish

The river was not far from the place we called town. It, our town, it was a dirty river town with a dirty river running through it. Town, it was mostly just a two-way road cutting through the middle of the place where the all-by-itself traffic light was always blinking from two sides of it yellow and from the other two sides of it red. Our town, us brothers one day discovered, it was not the kind of a town where cars not from our town liked to stop. Ours was a drive-on-through kind of a town, a pass-on-by-on-your-way-to-someplace-else kind of a town. Us brothers, we did not understand it why these cars from these other places would not want to stop to be and to stay with us. Look here: there was a dirty river in our dirty river town. There were dirty river fish in this here dirty river that us brothers liked to catch. There was a house, just up from this river, with a back-of-the-yard part where, us brothers, we liked to take the fish that we'd catch out of this dirty river and, us brothers, we liked to chop off the heads off of these fish. What we did then with the heads of these dirty river fish was this: we liked to take these fish's dirty river heads and we liked to give each of these fish heads each a name. Not one was called Jimmy or John. Jimmy and John, that was mine and my brother's name. We called each other Brother. What us brothers did after we gave each of these fish a name was, we liked to take these fish heads out back into the backest back part of the back of the yard, out back to where there was this pole back there sticking up toward the sky, the kind of a pole with electricity wires and telephone lines running down and running across to and into the rows of other peoples' houses where inside of these other houses there lived the other people of this dirty river town. This pole, it was covered, from its top to its bottom, with the chopped off heads that once belonged to our fish. Us brothers, we liked to hammer and nail them, these heads, open-eyed, open-mouthed, into this pole's blackened wood. When we did, with each swing of the hammer, these fish, it was like they were singing to us brothers. Brothers, these fish's fish mouths sang: Don't ever leave. We won't is what we promised to these singing fish. This, us brothers, we believed this, this would be an easy promise for us brothers to keep. And it was. It was—up until the day our father came home from work and told us we were leaving. When our father told us we were leaving, he meant it, we were leaving for good—this dirty river, this dirty river town. We did not want to leave, my brother and me. We did not want to leave behind this dirty river, this dirty river town. We did not want to leave behind this town or the river or the river's dirty river fish. We did not want to leave the fish-headed telephone pole out back in the back in our yard, back behind the wood tool shed where our father kept his hammers and his saws and those coffee cans of his full of rusty, bent-back nails. There was a bigger sky, our mother told us. There is a sky, our mother wanted us to know. There was a sky, she said, not stunted by smokestacks and smoke.

Us brothers, we couldn't picture a sky bigger than the sky outside our backyard. We did not want to imagine, we did not want to live in, a town without a dirty river running through it, a river for us to run down to it to fish. Us brothers, we did not want to run or be moved away from all of this smoke and water and mud. We liked dirt and mud and those dirty river smells that always smelled of fish and fishing and worms. We did not like it when our mother made us wash our hands to rid ourselves of those fishy river smells. Us brothers, we liked it the way the fishes' silver fish scales stuck to and glittered sparkly in our hands. At night, we liked to hold our hands up to the moonlight shining into our bedroom's window. Our hands, we believed, the brothers that we are, had been dipped in a river of stars. But us brothers, we didn't know what we were going to do, or how we were going to get ourselves to stay, until we looked outside and saw our fish. Those fish's heads, they were looking back at us brothers, they were singing out to us, Don't leave. A promise, the biggest fish head sang this out to us, is a promise. When we heard this fish's singing, us brothers, we gave each other this look. There was this look that us brothers, we sometimes liked to give each other this look. It was the kind of a look that actually hurt the eyes of the brother who was doing the looking. Imagine that look. Brother, Brother said to me then. Brother. We didn't have to say any other words other than this. This word brother, it was more than just enough. Outside, only the moon and the stars were watching us brothers as we climbed out through our bedroom's window and walked over to our father's tool shed and dug out his hammers and his coffee can filled with those rusty, bent-back nails. We each of us brothers grabbed a handful of nails and a hammer into each of our hands and then we walked over to our backyard's fish-headed telephone pole. Brother, I said to Brother. You get to go first. Give me your hand, I told him. Hold your hand up against this pole's wood. Brother did like I told. We were brothers. We were each other's voice inside our own heads. This might sting, I warned.

And then I raised back that hammer. I drove that rusted nail into Brother's hand. Brother didn't even wince, or flinch with his body, or make with his boy mouth the sound of a brother crying out. Good, Brother, I said. I was hammering in another nail into Brother's other hand when our father stepped out into the back of the yard. Son, our father called this word out. Us brothers— us, our father's sons—we turned back our boy heads toward the sound of our father. We waited to hear what it was that our father was going to say to us brothers next. It was a long few seconds. The sky above the river, the black metal mill shipwrecked down by the river's muddy shores, it was dark and quiet. Somewhere, we were sure, the sun was shining. You boys be sure to clean up out there before you come back in, our father said. Our father turned back his back. Us brothers turned to face back each other. I raised back that hammer. I lined up that rusted nail.

Our Father Who Walks on Water Comes Home with Two Buckets of Fish

This is our father we are watching. We watch our father walk on water. He is walking across it, our father, he is crossing this dirty river that runs through this dirty river town. Our father is coming back now from the river's other side. We see that he has, hanging from each of his muddy hands, a muddy bucket. When it is us, his sons, that he sees are the ones doing the watching, our father walks up to face us. He sets down those muddy buckets down onto the ground. Us brothers, we look down at those buckets. When we look down inside these buckets, we see that they are both filled up to the rusted brim with fish. Supper is what our father says to this. Us brothers, we shadow our father home. We are our father's sons mudding our way back through the mud, walking in the mud-left tracks of our father's muddy boots. When we get home, we watch our father walk into the kitchen without first taking off his boots. Us brothers, we do like our father. We walk inside, with our boots still on our feet. The floor, with mud all across it, it has never before looked so shiny. Mother, our father calls this word out. We listen to him call to our mother her name. Us brothers, we don't say anything about our mother. We go and we fetch a frying pan out of the cupboard and sit it down on the stove. Our father sees us brothers and so he gets for himself a knife for him to gut the fish with. Maybe what our father figures is that our mother is out of the house shopping. Our father takes the fish out of the buckets and he goes at the fish with his knife. He cuts off first the head, the tail next, then he sticks the rusted blade up inside. What is inside of this fish comes slushing out onto the kitchen's floor. We fry the fish up hard in sputtering hot butter, what our father likes to call lard. Boys, our father says, it's good to be back home. Then he calls out for our mother to come eat. When he gets no answer, only the rivery echo of a house with no mother left inside it, he keeps on eating. We keep on eating. Us brothers, we do not say a word about our mother. Our mother, our mother. We do not know what to say about our mother that our father doesn't already know. After we are done with this eating, it is us brothers who do the cleaning up. We take what is left off of our plates and we scrape what's left into the trash. The dirty dishes, slick with fish and lard, we pile these into the kitchen's sink. The parts of the fish that we do not eat—the guts, the heads, the bones—these we take outside, out back to the back of our backyard. The guts, the tails, these we bury, in holes that us brothers dig. The fish heads, with the fish eyes still staring out of them, these we hammer into the back-of-the-yard telephone pole that is studded with the heads of fish. It's the sound of us brothers doing this hammering that brings our father outside. When he asks us brothers, Where is your mother, one of us brothers whispers, Fish, and the other one of us mutters, Moon. To this, these words, our father, he nods with his head, then he heads back down to the river. And without so much as a word or a wave from his goodbye, we watch our father walk back across the river's muddy water, back to the river's other side: walking and walking and walking on, until he is nothing but a sound that the river sometimes makes when a stone is skipped across it.

The Hands that Hold the Hammer

Sometimes, us brothers, we hold our hands up to each other brother, and like this, with our hands raised in the air, us brothers, we tell each other what to do. Go get the hammer, one of our hands will say to the other brother. Go get us a handful of rusty, bent-back nails. Then meet me out back in the back of the backyard. One of us brothers will pick up with his picking-up hand the bucket of ours filled with fish. The other brother's hand will close up to make itself into a fist, its fish-out-of-water thumb sticking straight up and out from its hand to say to the other brother, Good, Brother, I'll meet you out back in the yard. Out back in the back of the yard, one brother's hand will say to the other brother who is doing the listening, Give me your hand. Hold your hand up against this pole's wood. Out back in our backyard, there is a telephone pole back there studded with the chopped off heads of fish. In the end there were exactly one hundred and fifty fish heads hammered and nailed into this pole's fish-headed wood. Us brothers, we gave each of these fish, each one of these fish's fish heads, each a name. Not one was called Jimmy or John. Jimmy and John was mine and my brother's name. We called each other Brother. Brother, one of our hands says. This might sting, the hand that is talking warns. And then the hand that is doing the warning, it raises back with the hammer it is holding and it drives the rusty, bent-back nail through skin and muscle and bone. The brother whose hand takes the nail through skin and muscle and bone, this is the brother who doesn't flinch, or wince with his body, or make with his boy mouth the sound of a brother crying out. Good, Brother, the hand that holds the hammer says. The hand that is holding the hammer and a handful of rusty, bent-back nails in its other brother hand, it takes his brother's other hand and holds this other hand back up against this backyard telephone pole's fish-head hammered in wood. This hand with the hammer held inside it, it lines up a second rusty nail for it to hit. But when this hammering hand raises back its hammer to hit, another hand from back behind us brothers raises up as if to tell us to stop. But this hand that is raising up from back behind us brothers' backs, it is not telling us brothers to stop. This hand that is raising up back behind us brothers, this hand that is pushing open and pushing out through our house's back-of-the-house door, it is the hand that is our father's. What our father's hand is saying, when it raises up like this, all it is saying to us is, You boys be sure to remember to clean up out here before you come back into the house. This house, it is our mother's house. Our mother, she is in the back of this house in a bed that has become her body. Us brothers, our hands, we hold them up, as high as we can hold them, to say to our father Okay, we'll clean up before we come back in. Us brothers, our boy hands, all four of them together, they could fit inside the fishing-man hands that are our father's. Our hands, like brothers, they close in toward each other. They raise back the hammer. They line up that rusted nail.

The Sound the Hammer Makes

This is us brothers at the age of what: two, three, five, one? Let's go back to us being the age we were when we were one. We are one and us brothers, we are just now beginning, we are just now learning, how to walk, how to talk, how to put the world into our mouths. Listen to us talk. What were our first words to come muddling up and out of our mouths? Was it Mama? Was it water? Was it mud, or river? Was it fish? This, know this, this is how the story of us brothers goes. This is us brothers down on our hands and knees, down by the river, with our fishing-man father. We are not, with our father, fishing. What we are doing is, us brothers, we are mucking around in the mud. This is us brothers lifting up our boy heads up from the mud here at the river's muddy edge. This is us looking up at the moon rising up and out of the river. This is us with our little boy mouths opening up to taste the taste of the muddy sky. Us brothers, us with our tongues, can you hear us, this is us saying the word fish. Even us at the age of one, even us before the age of one, us brothers, we see and us brothers we understand that the moon, it is a fish. Now, look at us brothers walking. On water? No, not quite yet. That'll come some years later. Now, we are holding the hands of our mother—imagine that!—we are holding the hands of our father, we are, us brothers, we are holding hands with each of us brothers. When we fall, these hands are the hands that pick us brothers up. Our father's hands are the hands that take us brothers out back into the back of our backyard, back to where there is a garage back there and a shed back there and a tree back there that does not have any branches, this tree, it doesn't have any leaves. What kind of a tree is this? Here, back here, on the dirt and grass ground that is our world, there are things back here for us brothers to stick inside our mouths. These here are things for us brothers to eat: the dirt, the grass, the mud, tree. This is how we go about learning about our world: what can and cannot be put inside our mouths, what we can and cannot eat—dirt and worms and grass and mud and those rusty, bent-back nails that fall to the ground from the curved black claw of our father's hammer. Back here too, in this backyard world, here is where us brothers will soon discover that dirt and grass, when it is wet outside, when it has been in the nighttime raining, the dirt turns into something other than dirt. When it rains, the dirt becomes better than dirt, it is magic to us brothers how dirt turns to mud. That word, mud, and muddy, and that other word that comes with it too: don't. These are the sounds that come muffing out at us brothers from the mouth that is our mother's. When our mother says to us brothers don't, no, mud, us brothers, we always end up doing, even back here then, what our mother has just told us brothers not to do. Maybe we do what our mother says for us brothers not to do—this no, this don't, this mud—because we like it when our mother and our father say to us these other words too: words that make the sound that a hammer sometimes makes when it hammers rusted nails into wood. You boys remember to clean up out there before you come back in. Years from us being one, us brothers, we will listen to that sound over and over again. Brother, we will say, to each other. Give me your hand. Hold your hand up against this wood. Us brothers will do what us brothers tell us to do. We are brothers. We are each other's voice inside our own heads. This might sting, us brothers will say to each other brother. Us brothers, we will raise back the hammer in our hand. We will drive that rusty, bent-back nail right through Brother's hand. Neither of us brothers will wince, or flinch, or make with our mouth the sound of a brother crying out. Good, Brother, Brother will say. Brother will be hammering in a second nail into us brothers' other hand when the father of us brothers will step out into the back of our backyard. Sons, our father will call this word out. Both of us brothers will turn back our boy heads toward the sound of our father to hear whatever it is that this father is going to say to us brothers next. It will be a long few seconds. The sky above the river where the steel mill sits shipwrecked in the river's mud, it will be dark and quiet. Somewhere, though, the sun will be shining. You boys be sure to clean up back here before you come back in, the father of us will say. This father will turn back with his voice and go back away into the inside of this house. Us brothers, we will turn back to face back with each other. Us brothers will raise back with our hammer, will line up that rusted nail.

Our Father Who Walks on Water Comes Home with Mud on His Boots

What our father is saying, what it is that our father keeps saying is, Where are my boots? Boots is what his mouth keeps on mouthing out. I took my boots off outside is what our father is saying, out back on the backyard steps is what he is telling us brothers what he did. I took them off just like your mother always tells us to do is how he explains it all to us. My boots, he says, they were covered in mud is why I took them off. But why? is what us brothers want our mouths to say to our father. But our father, he keeps on lipping with his lip. Where, where? is what he keeps asking. Where can my boots be? He looks at us, his sons, he looks to us brothers, as if we know the answer to this. Us brothers, we look back at our father but it is with a look that says that, us brothers, we don't know. Who is what our father wants to be told, who would walk off with a pair of beat-up boots? There were holes in the soles of those boots, our father tells us. Us brothers, we nod with our boy heads to let our father know that we know. We can picture in our boy heads the way the steel of the steel toe used to shine up from under the mud. We are boys shaking our heads at our father to let him know how sorry we are about his boots. We are with our heads the both of us brothers shaking when we look down to where our father's boots ought to be. There, where we are looking, there on our father's feet, us brothers, we see boots. We see our father's boots, all good and muddy, just like boots are meant to be. We see our father's boots right there where our father's boots are meant to be right there on our father's feet. What we say to our father is, Father, we say, look down. Down where? is what our father says to this, and what he does then is he looks around, he is looking up and down and all around, but where he doesn't look is down at his own two feet. Look down there, us brothers say, and we point down at his feet. You must've not took them off last night is what we tell our father is what most likely happened last night when he came home from a night with the river. It was a late night last night for our father and the river. We do not say to our father that we could hear him last night come into the house with his boots busting in through the back door smelling of river and whiskey and fish. What we do say to our father is something that us brothers, we find this funny for us brothers to imagine: it is funny for us brothers to even have to say. What we say is that it looks like to us brothers like maybe you wore your boots to bed. Our father's muddy boots, worn to bed, worn to a bed with our mother asleep in it—the thought of this, the picture of this in our boy heads: this, us brothers, we can hardly believe it. It must not have been our mother who was the mother asleep in the bed beside our father. Our mother, our mother would have made our father take off his muddy boots back at the back door, back before he came walking into the house. But our mother, our mother, she isn't our mother anymore. Our mother, asleep in bed, she is just this lump of a mother asleep in a bed with mud now dried in clumps upon its bedsheets. It, this bed, with this other mother asleep in it, it could be a bed made out of mud for all this other mother knows. Mud has got a hold of this mother now. This mother, she is this mother who is stuck in the mud now. And our father, with mud on his muddy boots, our father: he is walking on water now. He is walking back into our house. Sons, our father is saying. Our father, he is shouting out to us brothers, Boys, come here. Us brothers, us, our father's sons, we come running when we hear the sound of our father. Our father, his voice, it is a raised-back hammer hammering the backs of our boy heads. We run and we stop and we stand up tall. We are standing with our boot heels touching waiting to hear whatever it is that our father wants to say to us next. It is a long few seconds. Outside the window, the sky above the river, the sky above the river where the black-husked steel mill sits shipwrecked in the mud, it is dark and quiet. Somewhere, I am sure, the sun is shining. Your boots is what our father says to us brothers next. Boys, he tells us, let me take a good long look at your boots. Us brothers, we do what our father says. We lift up the legs of our muddy-legged trousers. We look down with our father. This is us, the three of us brothers, looking down at our mud-covered boots. When our father sees that crust of mud crumbling on the bottoms of our boots, our father does not say another word. He drops down, onto his hands and knees, down on the floor, and begins to eat.

What Our Father is Here to Tell Us

This is us brothers. This is us brothers doing what we are always doing. This is what we did. You: look here. See us brothers out back in the back of our backyard. We are cutting off the fish heads off of the fish that we have just fished out from the dirty river that runs its way through this dirty river town. And this here is our father. See our father, how he steps out back into the back of our backyard, and watch how he keeps stepping closer back toward where the two of us brothers are standing back here with our fish-cutting knives held in our hands until our father, he stops stepping back and then he just stands there for a while staring at what, us brothers, at what, his sons, what we are doing: us with our knives held in our hands, us brothers, us, our father's sons, us who are chopping off the heads off of our fish. This is us brothers doing what us brothers love to do best—us brothers fishing and us brothers getting all good and muddy and us brothers chopping off the heads off of our fish. And now, now look over there. There is a shed back here in the back of our backyard. This shed, it isn't made out of mud: it's made out of wood, what our father likes to call lumber, and us, our father's sons, we like it, the way that that word lumber, we like it how it comes lumbering out of his, out of our father's, mouth. And look: look. There is a garden back here too that is right now mostly just mud, just the way we like it. And there is a telephone pole too that is creosote-coated, this sticking-up-toward-the-sky pole that all up and down the sides of it us brothers have hammered and nailed into its black tar wood all of the fish heads that us brothers have cut off from all of the fish that we've fished out of the dirty river that runs its way through this dirty river town. Each of these fish heads each has been given by us brothers a name. Not one is called Jimmy or John. Jimmy and John is my brother's and my name. We call each other Brother. Our father, he calls us brothers Son. When our father hollers out to us brothers that word Son, the sound of it, that word, the way that it hangs in the air between us, it is a sound that we can't help but turn our heads to. When we hear that sound, us brothers, we both of us brothers know that we are crossing that river together. Son, we hear our father say to us now, our father, he who is right now staring at us brothers and he isn't saying anything more. Maybe there is nothing more for our father to say to us, his sons, than this word Son. But no. No, there *is* something more for our father to say to us, his sons, which is why he is out right now in the back of our backyard staring at us brothers with this stare that he is staring at us with. But what our father is about to say to us brothers, us brothers, we don't want to hear it. What it is he is about to say to us brothers, these sentences of his, they have words inside of them like leaving and going and for the best. After our father says what he says, our father tells us brothers that he, that we, that he and our mother, they don't expect us brothers to understand. Us brothers, we look at our father. We look up at and we look into his man's face and we nod with our boy heads because it's true. What we understand, now and forever, is that, us brothers, we won't ever understand—not now, not then, not ever. But this, we do not say this to our father, not with our mouths. We do not say this to our father's face. We'll save that for later. Now we just nod and we keep on with this nodding so that our father thinks that us brothers and our noddings means that, us brothers, we are okay with what he has said. Us brothers, we are not okay with what our father has just said to us brothers. But our father does not know that we are not okay with what he has just said. What our father does, to us brothers, to our nodding, is our father, he nods his head back. Good, Sons, our father says to us brothers, and then he turns away his face and starts walking back to our house with our mother there inside it. When the back door slams shut, us brothers, we know that now it is us brothers back to being just us. Us brothers, we turn to face off with each other. This is us brothers nodding our boy heads at nobody but us. Us brothers, we both of us know what it is that we have to do next. So we go, us brothers, not so slow, over to the backyard shed with our hands now hanging knifeless by our sides. When we come back out from the inside of this shed, in our hands now we are holding in them each a hammer and a handful of rusty, bent-back nails. Watch as us brothers walk this walk back to where our backyard's fish-headed telephone pole, it is a lit-up lighthouse shining in the moon's nighttime light. In the light of this light, see the two of us brothers take the other one of us by the hand. Brother, this might sting, Brother, the both of us brothers warn— we warn this to each other, we warn this to ourselves. Then the both of us brothers raise back with our hammering hands, we hold back our hammers. We line up those rusted nails.

We Make Mud

Look there at our father. Our father, see over there, he is digging, with his shovel, down into mud. He is, with this mud-crusted shovel, lifting the mud from over there where he is standing, hunched over, and he, our father, he is dumping the mud out, into a hump-mudded pile, here in this other not so muddy place, up here on this hill that is uphill from where the river is, up here where there is this grass up here that is trying to cover up the dirt that us brothers and now our father too—we like to take dirt and make dirt turn to mud. When us brothers ask our father, What is he doing, what our father says to this is, he says, he is working. Working? we say. We say this with our eyes. Work, no, work: work was back when our father used to have a work to go to, back when the black-metaled mill that now sits shipwrecked on the river's shore, so dark and silent, back when it wasn't so dark and silent, back when blast-furnace fire and smoking smokestack smoke used to make us brothers raise our eyes up to look up at the sky. But now that place where our father used to work, it is a shipwrecked ship with no treasures left inside it. Sons, our father says this to us. I'm making mud, he says. I'm taking mud, he tells us, and I'm making, with this mud, I am making, out of mud, a house for us to call our own. A mud house, our father calls it. A mud house where mud, it'll be okay for us to walk inside this house with mud caked on the bottoms of our boots. That sounds like a good place to us, us brothers, we say this to our father. And so, us brothers, being the good boys that we are, we drop down onto our hands and knees, down in the mud, and we get to work. We start at the bottom and make our way up. But a house, a house made out of mud, a mud house: this we do not make. Us brothers, what we make, from the mud, we make Girl. We make Girl's knees especially muddy. Girl's knees, they make us want to stay forever kneeling. It's when Girl stands up from the mud that's sticking to the skins of our muddy boy hands, it's then that we can see that Girl, she is naked. Brother is the brother of us brothers who is making Girl's nakedness seem like not such a good thing for Girl to be. So what if she's naked? That's what I've got to say to this. We're all naked underneath our clothes. But maybe, Brother says, maybe she's cold. Maybe she wants some clothes. Are you cold? I go and ask Girl. Would you like some clothes to put on top of your girl body? Girl doesn't say yes or no to this. She just stands there being naked. Brother turns though and runs away and when he comes back he has in his arms an armful of girl clothes. Where did you get those? I say this to Brother. Our mother's closet is what Brother says to this. I give Brother this look. There is this look that us brothers, we have this look between us brothers. It's the kind of a look that actually hurts the eyes of the brother who is doing the looking. Imagine that look. Where else was I supposed to look? Brother says. I don't know where or what to say to this, and so I don't say anything. I take back looking that look. Then I take hold of Brother's hand. I take out of Brother's hands this dress—it's a dress with yellow flowers on it: it is a dress that I cannot picture our mother ever wearing it, this dress—and then we slip, we tug, we pull, we fight, we struggle, we twist, we rip, this dress down over the top of Girl's head. Oh, even so, Girl is still beautiful. Girl's beauty—it shines—the beauty of mud, it is shining, from beneath our mother's flowery clothes.

The Dress with Girl Not in It

It's our mother's dress, the dress that us brothers slipped and tugged up and over the top of Girl's head, that night when we made Girl, made her out of the mud, made her up from the mud, us brothers, down by the river, down on our hands and knees, down in the river made mud—it is that same dress that is the dress that us brothers, we see it floating, a floating dead fish of a dress, floating down our dirty river, and Girl, Girl whose flowey dress this dress is, is nowhere to be found by it, or inside it, or nowhere even near it, this dress. Where's Girl? is what us brothers, the both of us, we want to know this. Where Girl is, this is one thing, Brother says. But what she is wearing, that is another thing too. What do you think Girl is wearing? I say to Brother. Not our mother's dress, Brother says back. Good, I tell him. I never did like it on her. It never did, I say, fit. It never did fit on Girl, Brother asks, or are you talking about on our mother? Both, I say to this. So do you think she's found another dress? Brother says. I think, I say back, that Girl is back to being the way that we made her. You mean she's back to being naked, then? Brother says. Yes, Brother, on this, Brother has got his mind set: his head, it is a head that is stuck in that naked girl kind of mud. So I say to Brother what Brother has heard me say more than twice before. I remind him that, we are all of us made naked under our clothes. This time, him hearing this, it gets Brother thinking: not about Girl being naked. What it gets Brother thinking about is our mother. You mean even our mother is naked underneath her clothes? Brother asks. Then Brother shoots me this look that, us brothers, we have these looks between us, and what this look says is, we don't want to think about that. I nod with my head and can't help it when my face makes one of those I've-just-bitten-into-something-that-tastes-really-awful kind of faces when I tell him: yes, Brother, even our mother is naked underneath her mother clothes. And then, the both of us brothers, we start up running as if we're running to run away from that naked mother kind of a place. But what we are really doing is we are running to that other made out of mud place where we think that Girl is most likely to be hiding out: upriver not too far, up where the mill sits in the mud like a shipwrecked ship that one day had run itself aground and then it didn't know where else for it to go. So it stayed. And men, men like our father, men who wear sun-yellow hard hats and carry rusty-steeled lunchbuckets packed with ham and cheese sandwiches, these men, they started filing, one by one, into the insides of this shipwreck of a ship and then they kept on coming in until smoke started funneling out through its smokestacked top and coke oven fires were iron ore stoked inside its black-metalled belly, and after a while coils of shining steel were being made on the inside of this place that had, once upon a time ago, it was a ship that had lost itself at sea. It is here, then, in the shadow of this, this ship, this mill where metal used to be made, this is where us brothers, that night, not too long ago, this is where we dropped down onto our hands and knees, down in the mud, and we made Girl. Here, out of river and dirt, us brothers, we made mud. We made Girl. In the mud, out of the mud, Girl was made naked. Even in the dark-of-night night, Girl's made-out-of-mud body shined, it shined like a thing brand new, it shined with the shine of the never-before-seen. Us brothers, our eyes, you should've seen our muddy boy eyes. Our eyes, brother: they became moons, that night. Then lighthouses. Then they became hands that taught us that to touch a thing so beautiful you can only touch it once. Twice, touch it twice, and its beauty will banish you with its beauty. Brother, Brother's eyes, his were the muddy hands that did not know how just to look: not touch. We gotta get Girl dressed was what Brother said, because Brother knew what his right hand was wanting to reach up and do. She's cold, Brother said. But no, it was not cold, that night. That night, the mud was hot to our boy touches: it was this melty thing melting in our muddy boy hands. But Brother's head, his boy head was now set on getting Girl dressed. So Brother left and when he came back he was holding in his arms an arm full of girl clothes. Where'd you get those? is what I wanted to be told. So what Brother told me was, From our mother's closet. Our mother's closet? I did not even have to say it, those three words. What I did was I gave Brother another one of those looks that us brothers had between us: it was the kind of a look that actually hurt the face of the brother who was doing this looking. Imagine that look. But where else was I supposed to look? was what Brother had to say. I didn't know. I didn't know what to say to this. So, I took back that look. But you, look right now. Look away from looking at us brothers, and look to the river, look so that you can see the dress that is now slowly floating down the river away. This dress is yellow. No, that's not right: this dress is a kind of blue. It is brown. It is the color the water is. It is a fish—it is a fish that has forgotten how to swim: it is a fish floating across a muddy river sky. Now, it is a kite now. Now, it is a star. No, now, what this is is, it is a dress with no one inside it. It is blowing, it is floating, it is going away. The wind, the river, it is taking it away from us brothers who are down here by the river trying to get us a look. If it looks like there is a girl inside of this dress: look closer. There is no girl there inside it. This dress, it is just a dress, it is girl-less. But Girl. You know: Girl. Girl is another story. Us brothers, we know where to go to go see Girl. Girl is out in the river, she is out standing out in the middle of the river, standing with her girl legs spread wide open at the hips so that ships cutting up the river going to places up the river, up beyond our dirty river town, upriver to where there are these city lights shining up there even though, through all the mud and smoke, us brothers, we cannot see them—Girl is standing in such a way, out in the river, so that the river's muddy water is just barely touching her knees. Girl's knees are especially muddy. Girl's knees are knees that when we made them, us brothers—we wanted to remain forever in the mud kneeling. Girl's knees were that muddy. Look: you can see them now. You can see more than that now. Girl is back now to being just mud. That is to say, Girl is back to being the way that we made her, back to being the way she was made to be: naked, bare, pure: pure mud. Us brothers, when we see Girl standing out in the middle of the river, the all of Girl, the full moon of Girl for all our eyes to see, to see her the way that Girl was meant to be seen—naked, naked, nude, nude— what we do is we run ourselves up to Girl, we are running up through and into the shadow of Girl—the shadow of Girl, it is a muddy cloud that is closing in on top of us brothers: it is a big-mouthed fish teaching us littler fish how to fly—this is us brothers fishing our way up toward that mouth, out and up to where Girl is standing: us brothers, we are stones skipped across the river's water: this muddy river, it is a road that does not have a name. It does not have a name so, us brothers, we decide to name it. We decide to name it the same way we gave names to every one of those dirty river fish that us brothers used to fish out of this dirty river that runs through this dirty river town. No, we do not call this road Jimmy or John. Jimmy and John is mine and my brother's names. We call each other Brother. This road, this dirty river, this dirty river road—us brothers—we decide to call it Girl. When we call this road Girl, this dirty river of a road throws out its mud carpet for us brothers to walk across it. Us brothers, we do not walk across it. We run across it. We run and run until we are run out of river, until we are running half the way up the leg that is the muddy leg of Girl. Girl's mud leg is a ladder that ladders us brothers up, up to where Girl's head, it has punched a hole into the blue of the sky. We are looking Girl right in the eye now. There is an eye for each of us brothers. Girl's eyes are on the other side of the sky now. Girl's eyes are moons. Girl's eyes are even bigger than that other moon that you all know about, you know, that other moon that you see floating in the sky when you look at night out the window—that moon, you could reach out and hold that other moon in the palm of your hand. That's how small it is compared to how big Girl's eyes are when you look at them like this and see into them the way they were meant to be seen, this way up close. What are you doing here? is what us brothers say to Girl when we get beyond this way of looking. We ask this, no, not to find out what is Girl doing standing mud-naked in the middle of the river. We know what she is doing when Girl is doing that. What we want to know is, what is Girl doing with her hands. In her girl hands, Girl is holding what could be a ball of snow—it is that white. It could be, if the light was right, if it was night out instead of day, you might be made to believe that in her hands Girl was holding the moon. Or maybe she is molding the moon back to being full. But believe this when we tell you this, in Girl's hands, what looks to be a ball of snow, or a moon—it isn't. What it is is, it is a ball made out of cloud. And Girl, Girl is rolling, she is pinching these white yarny pieces of cloud in between her I've-got-a-gun finger and her trigger-of-a-gun thumb. And Girl, she is doing with these linty pieces of gathered-up cloud what our mother used to do back in the whiteness of winter—days when she'd needle us wool sweaters that never did fit us stitched from rolls of itchy yarn. I am making myself a dress is what Girl tells us brothers is what she is doing. Why on earth, is what I am thinking, would Girl want to wear a dress? Girl is perfect just the way she is, with no dress on to cover up her mud. To put a dress on this, on top of this, over this—this would be, in this brother's eyes, wrong: it would be just plain bad: it would be dumb, dumb, dumb. It would be like if the moon were to one night rise into the night's sky wearing a black dress on to keep its light from reaching the earth. That too would be dumb. But Girl is not dumb. Girl knows what is good and what is bad. So what I want to know is, What is Girl thinking? What has gotten into Girl's head? And so this is what I ask her. What, I say, are you thinking? Why would you want to make for yourself a dress? Our mother's dress: that was Brother's bad idea. But this, to this, Girl reaches out to me and she takes me up in her hand. She takes me up into her girl hand and then she takes my hand and she tells me to feel. My hand, it reaches out and it touches the part of Girl's body where Girl has just now told me to feel. This is where Girl's heart is. I can feel it, the beat of this heart, that made-out-of-mud drum, beating there beneath the mud of Girl's skin. But Girl's skin— this, I must tell you this: it is like the river is when the river freezes over. It is that cold: it is ice. And so, when I reach my boy hand up and in to take hold of Girl's heart, to warm it up, to hold it up close to my own boy heart, this heart that is Girl's, this heart that is made out of mud, this heart that is shaped like a fish: when I touch it—this heart—it shatters into a billion pieces. Each broken piece becomes a star.

What the Fish of the River Tell Us to Do

In our room, at night, in the dark, us brothers, we do not sleep. What we do, at night, in our room, in the dark, is we stare out our bedroom's window. Through our bedroom's window, us brothers, we can see out back into the back of our backyard. Out back in the back of our backyard, us brothers, we can see our fish. We can see the fish, we can see those fishes' heads, fish heads that are hammered and nailed, with rusty, bent-back nails, into our back-of-the-yard telephone pole. This back-of-the-yard telephone pole, it is studded with the chopped off heads of fish. These fish heads used to be fish with fish bodies living in the dirty river that runs its way through this dirty river town. Our town, it is a dirty river town with a dirty river running through it. Those fishes' heads, they stare back at us brothers, open-eyed, open-mouthed, and it's like they're singing to us brothers. When these fish sing like this to us, us brothers, we listen to what these fish say. What the fish say to us brothers, when they sing like this to us, they say, Brothers, don't leave. It was our father's voice, it was our father who came home from work that day and told us we were leaving. When our father told us we were leaving, our father, he meant it, we were leaving for good: this dirty river, this dirty river town. Us brothers, we did not want to leave. We did not not want to leave behind this dirty river town or this dirty river where us brothers always liked to run down to it to fish. We did not want to leave behind the fish-headed telephone pole out back in the back of our backyard. There were exactly one hundred and fifty fish heads hammered and nailed and singing out to us brothers from the split black wood of that backyard telephone pole. We gave each of these fish each a name. Not one was called Jimmy or John. Jimmy and John was my and my brother's name. We called each other Brother. Brother, I liked to say. Brother, I said, the night our father told us we were leaving. Give me your hand. Let's show those fish how we're going to keep ourselves from going away. Stay, I said, to Brother. Stand right here is what I said to him then, and then I walked with Brother out back into the back of our yard. Out back in the back of our backyard, that backyard telephone pole, it was sticking up, it was standing up, like the backbone of some stuck-in-the-mud fish. When I said to Brother, Give me your hand, Brother did like I told. He gave me his hand. I held Brother's held out hand back up against the wood of this fish-headed backyard telephone pole. In my other hand, I was holding onto our father's hammer. In my mouth, I was holding with my teeth a couple of our father's rusty, bent-back nails. This might sting, I said to Brother. And then I raised back with that hammer. I drove that nail right through Brother's hand. Brother didn't flinch, or wince with his body, or make with his mouth the sound of a brother crying out. Good, Brother, I said. I was hammering in another nail into Brother's other hand when our father stepped out into the back of the backyard. Boys, our father called out to us brothers. Us brothers, we turned with our boy heads back toward the sound of our father. We waited to hear what it was that our father was going to say to us brothers next. It was a long few seconds. The sky above the river where the steel mill stood shipwrecked in the river's mud, it was dark and silent. Somewhere, I was sure, the sun was shining. You boys be sure to clean up before you come back in, our father said to us then. Our father turned back his back. Us brothers, we turned back to face back each other. I raised back the hammer. I lined up that rusted nail.

Stones that Float

There are stones along this river's muddy bank that do not sink. They float, though in us brothers' hands, these stones, they feel heavy to us brothers—feel the way that we believe stones should feel: hard, solid, things made from the dirt to be out over the dirt thrown. Throw them into the river, though, and these stones become boats that float on top of the river. Us brothers, we don't know what to believe when we see a thing like this happen. This hasn't always been the way with us brothers and stones. There was a time when, us brothers, we remember stones that used to sink. We'd throw them up and above and into the river and watch them disappear. In the darkness of the river we'd hear these stones go plunk and plunk. Maybe now it's the river and not the stones. Maybe it's that the river is more mud than it is water now, and the stones that we are throwing aren't really floating. Maybe what these stones are doing is, they are just sitting there the way that stones sometimes sit in the mud: sit, and sit, for years, for centuries, until us brothers come walking up and along the river's muddy shore and reach down with our muddy boy hands to pick the stones up from the mud. We pick the stones up from the mud so that we can throw them, so we can see a stone in flight, can stand and watch this thing without any wings rise above this earth.

We Eat Mud

Us brothers, we kept reaching down, with our hands, down into the mud. We kept on with our hands reaching down, into the mud, and when we did, us brothers, we kept on pulling up mud. But then once, when we reached with our hands down into the mud, us brothers, we pulled up Girl. We pulled Girl up, out of the mud, until Girl became a tree. Us brothers, up this girl tree, up, us brothers, we climbed. We climbed up this girl tree that used to be Girl, this tree that used to be mud, until us brothers got up to this tree's top. Up here, at the top of this tree, us brothers, out of tree branches and tree leaves, all the color of mud, we made us a nest. In the sky above our heads, there was a cloud up there in the shape of a bird. This cloud, it was so shaped like how a bird is shaped that it became, it turned into, it was: a bird. This bird, it flew over to where, us brothers, we were standing up watching with our heads lifted up to see. When this bird that was once a cloud was close enough for us to touch it, us brothers, we reached out with our hands to touch it. We touched it. We touched this bird that was once a cloud once shaped in the shape of a bird, and when we did, this bird, it started singing. Then, this bird, this bird that, it was singing, then it and its singing, it flew away. When it came back, this bird, a little while later, like a good bird that always comes back, its bird mouth was filled with mud. This bird, with its bird mouth filled up with mud, this bird, it wasn't singing. What this bird did, even though it wasn't a bird singing to us brothers anymore, it flew back up close to us brothers above us our boy heads. Us brothers, looking up at this bird, we opened up our boy mouths. When we did this with our mouths, this bird, it opened up its mouth too, it started back up singing. And like this, with mud dripping down from this bird's singing mouth and down into ours, us brothers, we began to eat.

Fish Heads

It was a good day of us brothers fishing. It was always a good day of us brothers fishing whenever us brothers went down to the river to go do us our fishing. It was a good day of us brothers going down to the river to go do us our fishing even when us brothers didn't catch us many or any of those dirty river fish that live in the dirty river that runs through this dirty river town. But this day was not one of those days of us brothers not catching us many or even any fish. This day, us brothers, we fished out of the dirty river that runs through this dirty river town more fish than us brothers, with our mother and our father both sitting down at the table with us brothers, we caught us brothers more fish this day than the four of us in our house could in one sitting sit down and eat. It was one of those kinds of fishing days, that day, down at the river that day. Our buckets, that day, they couldn't hold down inside of them all of our dirty river fish. Us brothers, we had to twice run down, with our buckets, back down to the dirty river that runs through this dirty river town for us brothers to bring back up to the back of our backyard all of that day's dirty river catch. But the trouble, that day, with all of this was this: that when we got back to the back of our backyard that day with our buckets twice filled up to their muddy brims with fish, us brothers, we couldn't find where our fish-cutting knives were that we used to gut and to cut off the heads off of our fish. Our fish-cutting, fish-gutting knives, they were nowhere to be, by us brothers, found. Us brothers, we usually kept these knives that were ours down inside the front pockets of the muddy-kneed trousers that us brothers always pulled on us in the morning. But when we fished our boy hands down inside of our trouser's pockets, all we fished back up into our fists was the lint at the bottoms of these pockets. There was enough lint between us brothers, in our fists, that day, for us brothers to fly a kite with. But us brothers, we didn't want us to fly us a kite that day. What us brothers wanted to do, that day, was we wanted to do with our fish what we always did with our fish. Us brothers, once we fished these fish that were ours out of the dirty river that runs through this dirty river town, we liked to take these fish out back to the back of our backyard, out back to where there was a telephone pole back there, back behind our father's shed, that was studded with the chopped off heads of fish. Each fish, each fish head, us brothers, we gave each one a name. Not one was named Jimmy or John. Jimmy and John was mine and my brother's name. We called each other Brother. Brother, Brother said, when we both of us looked and saw that both of us could not find inside of our trouser's pockets our fish-cutting knives. What are we going to do? Brother said. How, was what Brother wanted to know, are we going to gut and cut off the heads off of our fish? When Brother said what he said, about our knives and our fish, I gave Brother a look. There was this look that us brothers, we sometimes liked to look at each other with this kind of a look. It was the kind of a look that actually hurt the eyes of the brother who was doing the looking. Imagine that look. Look, I told Brother this. Brother, look inside. Brother turned, then, when he heard what I said, and he went inside our house, in through the back door, and into our mother's kitchen, to go looking inside there to see if he could find us our fish-gutting, fish-head-cutting knives. When Brother came back outside, a little while later, Brother was holding in both of his boy hands the kind of a knife that you use to butter your bread with. Brother, I said to Brother. Hold out your hands, I told him. Hand me over those knives. Brother did just like I told. We were brothers. We were each other's voice inside our own heads. And so I took those knives out from Brother's held-out hands, and then I threw them, hard and down, so that both of these knives stuck themselves down into the ground's not-so-hard dirt. You can't cut off a fish's head, I said to Brother, with this kind of a knife, I said. That would take us all day was what I told him. Brother looked, then, and said to this, then, Brother, what's the hurry? I looked back at Brother, once again, with our look. I looked him all over with this look. Brother, I said to Brother. Come with me, I said. And I walked my brother out back to the backest part of our backyard, out back to where our fish, our fish heads, they were with their open mouths, their open eyes, they were singing to us brothers. Brother, I said to Brother. Open up your mouth, I told Brother. Brother did like I told. We were brothers, remember. We were each other's voice inside our own heads. Now, close your eyes shut, I told Brother this. And here again, Brother did what he was told. Good, Brother, I said. Brother did not, with his eyes closed shut like this and with his mouth opened up wide, see me reach my hand into one of our buckets and fish me out one of our fish. I held this fish, fish-head first, out toward my brother. Then I stuck that fish into Brother's open mouth. Like this, fish after fish, opening and closing his mouth like this, Brother, us brothers, we chopped off these fishes' heads.

Fish Heads: Revisited

Then there was the time, us brothers, we fished a fish out from the dirty river that runs its way through this dirty river town, and this fish, inside of this fish, when we stuck up our knives up inside of this fish, to gut the guts out of this fish, this fish, up inside of this fish, there was a fish head up inside of this fish with a rusty, bent-back nail running through this fish's eye. This fish head is one of ours, was what I said to this. What Brother said back to this was, How do you know it's one of ours? The nail, I said, to Brother saying this. How many fish heads in this world have a rusty, bent-back nail running through it? What Brother said back to this was, How many? I took hold of this fish with this fish head stuck up inside of it, and I held it up close for Brother to take a closer look. Look, I said. This here fish head stuck up inside of this here fish with this rusty, bent-back nail running through its eye, this is it, this is the only one, this is the one and only, this fish head, I'm telling you, this fish head, it belongs to us. Brother looked at this fish and then he looked at me back straight in the eye like I was a brother who was lying. Prove it, was what Brother said. Prove it? I said to Brother then. You want me to prove it to you that this fish head is one of ours? Brother nodded his boy head. I took this fish which had this fish head stuck up inside of it and I shook its fish tail in Brother's face. You want me to prove it? I'll prove it, I said. I said, to Brother then, Give me your hand, Brother. Brother did like I told. He held out his hand for me to take it. We were brothers. Up until now, we were each other's voice inside our own heads. Good, Brother, I said. Us brothers, like this, hand in hand, we walked up away from the river back to our up-from-the-river house, then we walked out back into the back of our backyard. Out back in the back of our backyard, back here there was a telephone pole back here studded with the chopped off heads of fish. Look, I said to Brother, and I held his hand up against this fish-headed telephone pole. See that space right up there in the middle of all these other fish heads, I said. You see where that space is. There used to be a fish's fish head up in there in that empty space. Brother looked but didn't see what I wanted him to see. How do you know this? Brother said to this. Maybe you just *think* there used to be a fish's fish head up there in that empty space. I held onto Brother's hand then tighter than I'd ever held it before. I know it used to be there, I said, because I nailed it there myself. Just like this. And just like this, I reached back with my hammering hand, I raised back with my hammer, I drove a rusty, bent-back nail through Brother's hand. Brother didn't wince, or flinch with his body, or make with his boy mouth the sound of a brother crying out. Good, Brother, I said. I was about to hammer in another nail into Brother's other hand when our father stepped out into the back of our backyard. Sons, our father called this word out to us. Us, our father's sons, we turned back our boy heads toward the sound of our father. We waited to hear what words our father was going to say to us brothers next.

It was a long few seconds. The sky above the river where the steel mill stood shipwrecked in the river's mud, it was dark and quiet. Somewhere, I was sure, the sun was shining. You boys remember to clean up out here before you come back in, our father said to us then. Our father turned back his back. Us brothers turned back to face back with each other. I raised back the hammer. I lined up that rusted nail.

Burning Up

Us brothers are out back, we are out back in the back of our backyard, burning leaves with our backyard father, when Brother turns back around to face off with our father to ask our father does he know if mud will burn. Our father shrugs with his shoulders and grunts that he doesn't know if mud will burn or not, says, We'll have to wait ourselves to see. But wait: us brothers, we have been waiting and wanting to see things burn for quite a long time now, ever since the smokestacked mill sitting black and silent on our dirty river's dirty rivershore stopped setting fire to that dirty river sky that holds this dirty river town below it down in its dirty river place. The sky here in this dirty river town, it has been raining so many rivers of late, so much mud and rain and thunder, that when we do set fire to the raked up leaves that us brothers, we have raked them into leafy piles here in the back of our backyard, heaped back in the mud that used to be our mother's garden, what the heaped-up leaves do is they most just sit there and smoke—these leaves: they do not burn. And so that night, after our father has gone back inside of our house and has gotten himself all undressed and then redressed for his going to bed sleeping and is then sound asleep in bed, our father with our mother, a wadded-up lump of clothes in bed beside him, what I do is I whisper to Brother, through the late-night hushness of our room, Brother, let's go see. See what? is what Brother mumbles with his mouth mushing up against his pillow. See, I say to Brother, if the mud will burn or not, I say. I say it real slow, and I hold up for Brother's eyes to see a boxful of matchsticks, and then I strike up a matchstick so that Brother can better see. Your face, Brother tells me. It is a half of a moon is what Brother says. Good, Brother, I say to him back. What I can see now, here in this light, is that Brother, he is right here with me in what we both want ourselves to go see. Let's go, Brother, I say, and I let the matchstick's fire burn down until it burns down to the tips of my dirty boy fingers. Back outside, the moon's other half, the moon's other half brother, it is a moon that is fully glowing. There is a fire that burns inside the moon. There is a light inside of that lighthouse. Even a brother born blind would be able to see this. Now, see this for yourself: us brothers, out in the moon's cut-in-half light, we go out to our father's backyard shed, out to where our father keeps his muddy buckets and muddy shovels, his wood-rot ladders and those tools of his too big to keep in a box, and what we do inside of this outside place is we tiptoe up and then lower on down from where it is sitting, rusting half the way up on its shelf, a steel gas tank filled up inside with gasoline. It, this gas-filled tank, it is mostly full, and it is heavy, and so we lug it together, the two of us brothers, out back into the back of our yard, back to where our mother's garden, it is mostly just mud and leaves. What us brothers do next is, we screw off the gas can's rusted lid and we walk with it in a circle out around the weedy edge of the garden, tilting it like so so that the liquid inside it slowly pizzles out. When this can is good and empty of all that was inside it, I fish out two matchsticks out of the matchstick box and I turn around to stand face to face with Brother. Watch this, I say to Brother's face, and I drag each matchstick along the strip of sandpapery black that runs along the sides of this box. The red tips of the matchsticks turn redder now with fire. I reach out and hand one of these lit matchstick matches over to Brother's reaching out hand. The empty gas can, I take this out of Brother's other hand. Now listen: there are a few things us brothers can do with these matchsticks burning in our boy hands. We could, with our blowing-out breath, blow the lit matchsticks out. We could, too, with a quick flick of our wrists, just like this, snuff the matchstick fires black. Or—and this is what we do do—we could drop the lit up matchsticks into the mud to see what happens: to see if the mud is going to burn. So watch this: when we drop, on the count of one, two, three, our lit up matchsticks into the mud, the mud catches fire with a hiss. This hissing, it is a sound that us brothers, we have never heard mud make this sound ever before. Listen with us now to this mud burning. The mud, it is alive now with flame and with fire. No, Brother, there is nothing slow and just smoking away about the way that this fire is burning. Us brothers, we are jumping back now just to keep our boots from catching on fire. The mud, it is good and it is burning. Brother, it is on fire! Us brothers, we raise up our dirty boy hands up to the fire to keep the light from this fire from burning, from frying up, from boiling hard, our boy eyes up. Watch out, we say to each other brother, and we each of us brothers take two steps back and from the fire away. We keep taking more and more steps, back and then back, to keep this fire, this burning up mud, away from the both of us. We only do stop taking steps back and away from these burning up flames when we hear the sound of our father. It is his voice that is calling out to us brothers this word that he calls us, Son. Us, our father's sons, when we hear our father calling this word out to us brothers, us brothers, we always stop and drop what it is we are doing to see why our father is calling us out. Our father, we see, when we turn toward the sound that he is making with his mouth, we see that he is standing, boxed in, framed, hung is what it looks like to us, by the opening of our house's back door. Our father's face, his head, his whole man body, it is all lit up with the mud's burning up light. See, our father is saying to us then, he is nodding at us brothers with his head. Us brothers, we can see. Us brothers, we can feel the fire closing in closing behind us. We nod, too, back at our father, but move, us brothers, we do not do. Our boots, us brothers, we are stuck here in this mud. We are waiting. Us brothers, we are watching to see. What did I tell you. This is what our father says to us. Patience is the word that he says. Patience, this is us brothers being patient. My boy hands, where it is holding onto the gas can's rusted metal handle, it is good and it is heating up. When it blows, us brothers, we do not feel a thing. After, when we look back down on all of this burning up mud, what we see is our father: our father, he is down on his man hands and man knees, down in the mud and dirt and leaves, and he is trying, with his hands, to pick us brothers, us sons, up. But what our father doesn't know is this. Us brothers, we are up in smoke now. Us brothers, we are brothers rising in the sky now. This is us brothers burning up.

Good, Mother

Our father is not with us.

Our father isn't with us, but our mother, we know, is, so us brothers go into our house to see her.

Mother, we say. Mother.

Our mother says the word, What.

She says what twice.

Once for each of us brothers.

It's time for bed, we say.

Us brothers, we say this just once.

We each of us brothers take hold of one of our mother's hands. We walk like this, with our mother, back into the back of our house, back to where the back bedroom is where our mother and our father both go to go to sleep, back to where they both sometimes go when they want to be away from the other.

We lay our mother down into this bed.

Into this bed, our mother, she lays her body down.

When our mother is one with this bed, us brothers, we pull the covers up and under her chin.

Our mother's hands, our mother, she folds them into each other on top of where her rising up and down with breath chest is hiding underneath the bed's bed-sheet.

Sleep good, Mother, us brothers say.

Us brothers go outside, then, into the dark, out back into the back of our yard, back where our father's shed is with our father's tools, his nuts and bolts and screws, his hammers and nails, his mud-rusty buckets and sharp-toothed saws, and those bottles of his half-filled up with whiskey.

Only us brothers know what we are going outside to get: for us to get what we need us to get for our mother to not want to take us away from this dirty river place.

The river.

The fish.

Our fish-headed telephone pole.

The mud that us brothers love to make.

Our mother.

When we come back in, us brothers, in our hands, we are both of us holding in each one of our hands a hammer and a handful of rusty, bent-back nails.

We go back inside back to where our mother is back there in bed doing what looks to be sleeping.

Our mother, we see, she is not sleeping.

Our mother's eyes are moons in a mud-blackened sky.

Our mother's bed is a held-out hand with a body that is our mother's held up in it.

Our mother who does not know what it is she is saying when she is saying to us brothers that there is a sky not stunted by smoke.

Our mother who always made us brothers wash the mud from our hands and from off the bottoms of our muddy boots.

Our mother who said to us brothers that she wanted to go somewhere, anywhere was the word she said, so long as anywhere was west of here.

West where? was what our father wanted to know.

West of all this muddy water was what our mother said.

Somewhere, our mother said to us brothers, where there's not so much mud and smoke and steel.

Us brothers, we couldn't picture a sky bigger than the sky outside our backyard. We did not want to imagine a town without a dirty river running through it where we could run down to it to fish. Us brothers, we did not want to run or be moved away from all of this smoke and water and mud.

Mother.

Look here.

Our mother, she is ours.

Us brothers'.

We kneel ourselves down by the side edge of our mother's bed.

If it looks as if we are praying, take a look again.

Us brothers, what we are doing is, we are taking our mother by the both of her hands, and then we take these hands that are our mother's, we take these hands that we are holding, and then we hold them back up against the back part of this bed, back where our mother's head, it is now resting back up against this bed's mud-colored wood.

Or is it lumber?

This might sting, us brothers warn.

Us brothers, we give each other this look.

There is this look that us brothers, we sometimes like to look at each other with this look. It is the kind of a look that actually hurts the face of the brother who is doing the looking.

Imagine that look.

Brother, one of us brothers says, you can go first.

No, you can go, Brother.

Then: let's both of us both go both of us at the same time.

Us brothers, we both nod with our boy heads yes. Then we raise back our hands that are holding these hammers, and then we hammer those rusty, bent-back nails right through our mother's hands.

Our mother doesn't wince, or flinch with her body, or make with her mouth the sound of a mother crying out.

Good, Mother, we say.

Us brothers, we are hammering in two other nails into both of our mother's hands when our father walks into the room.

Boys, our father says.

When we hear this word boys, us brothers, we turn back with our boy heads toward the sound of our father.

We wait to hear what it is that our father is about to say to us brothers next.

It is a long few seconds.

Outside the window, the sky above the river where the steel mill sits shipwrecked in the mud, the sky is dark and silent. Somewhere, I am sure, the sun is shining.

You boys be sure to be careful, our father says to us, not to wake up your mother up from her sleep.

Our father turns back his back.

Us brothers turn back to face back our mother.

Our mother's eyes look up at us brothers, but we cannot tell you what it is that they see.

Us brothers, look at us brothers: we raise back the hammer.

We line up these rusted nails.

Burning Up: Revisited

This house, our house, it is a dark house when us brothers are not inside it. Our mother, she likes to keep this house this way, with the lights inside unlit around her. At night, when us brothers go outside to go down to the river fishing, we like to leave with the lights in our house left on burning. We like to picture this, our mother, pushing up from her bed to make the lights in the house go dark. But one night, when us brothers leave with the lights in our house still glowing, we see, three hours later, when we are making our way back home from the river, we see that the lights in our house, there is this other kind of a light burning out from inside of our house. Our house, as we make our way even closer to it, we see that our house, with our mother there inside it, it is burning up on fire. There is this other kind of light shining out from around our house. This light, it is the light of fire. Come on, us brothers, we say this to each other, and then we run in our boots back to our on-fire house. In our muddy brother hands, us brothers, we have our muddy buckets hanging and banging up against our boy hips. Our buckets are filled up the rims of them with fish. Us brothers, we run with these muddy buckets filled up with fish and we do not stop with this running until we are within a muddy bucket's throw of our house. When we run ourselves out of breath running home like this, we give each other this look. There is this look that we have between us brothers. It is the kind of a look that actually hurts the eyes of the brother who is doing the looking. Imagine that look. This look, with this look, what it says to the brother who isn't doing the looking is, What should we do now? Us brothers, we know what we should do now. We should run with our muddy buckets back down to the muddy river to bucket up into our buckets some muddy river water for us to throw onto our house. But us brothers, we can see the looks of our house, that it is too late for us to do this. This would do us, our house, with our mother there inside it, no good. So what we do do is, we do this: we take what is down inside our buckets—the fish that we have fished out of the dirty river that runs through this dirty river town—and we take these fish and we hold these fish by the heads of these fish up close to the fire. These fish, they are still alive and gilling at the sky for air. The fins of these fish, finning upwards in our hands, they are still kicking. But alive, these fish, alive these fish are not alive for long. Not if it is up to us. And it is up to us. It doesn't take long for these fish to cook up good and smoky. Us brothers, we know that these fish are done being cooked when we hear our mother's voice calling out from the inside of our house telling us brothers that something is on the stove burning. Boys, our mother says. What's that smell? We got it, Mother, us brothers, we holler this out to our mother from this side of the fire. Don't you worry, we say. Go back to sleep, we say. It's just us cooking up our fish. Then us brothers, we say to our mother, that we're going back down to the river, we say, to go fish us up some more fish, we say, but this time, we tell her, we'll be sure to turn out all the lights.

The Sky at the Bottom of the River

There are people here in this town, in this dirty river town with this dirty river running through it, who will be quick to tell you that what happened to our father, when he walked out into the river, was that he, our father, in the river, drowned. But us brothers, we are here to tell you this: that our father, when he walked out into the river, no, our father, he did not die. He lived is what our father did. Our father was saved, that night, when he walked out into the river, when he walked out across the river's muddy water. Yes, our father, he is right now safe and sound and he is more than just alive, down on the bottom of this dirty river, down here where the rest of this dirty river's dirty river fish live like the dirty river fish that these fish are and will always in the river be. Us brothers, we go to see and to be with our father on those nights when the river's other dirty river fish aren't, for us brothers, biting. Those other dirty river fish, we tell this to ourselves, we tell this to each other, they must be hanging out, these fish must be hanging down, down at the muddy bottom of the muddy river's bottom. And so, on nights like this, us brothers, what we do is this: we take two deep breaths down inside of our boy mouths, and us brothers, like this, we dive down to the river's bottom. Us brothers, here in the river, down where the water down here is thick and dirty with mud and river and fish, the way we like it to be, us brothers, see, we can breathe. When we open up our boy mouths, this river's muddy water, it turns to air. It is like this with our father, too. Our father, he was the one of us who taught us brothers how to under the river's muddy water breathe. Breathe in is what our father told us, the first time we came down to the river to see him, down here at the river's bottom. Don't worry about breathing, our father to us brothers said. All you got to do is believe. Believe what? was what Brother wanted to know. And what our father said to this was, Believe in the river, he said. Don't you see, our father asked us. Our father said, The river is like sky. Then he told us to dive inside. Us brothers, we sometimes do what it is we are told. And so, dive inside, this we did. When we did, when we dove head-first down into the river, the river shattered into a billion pieces. Each broken piece became a star.

Girl Breathes a River

There is a river flowing inside Girl's body that floats up out of Girl whenever Girl breathes. Brothers other than us might say, that's no river, that's just some girl breathing out her girl breath, but us brothers who made Girl and us brothers who believe Girl, we know a river when a river's what we see. No, yes, us brothers, we know better than to say no to what we see and what we say and what we believe to be true. So what us brothers say instead of us saying no is we say Girl. We hop up on board of our made-out-of-mud boat and we oar our way down along this muddy river that flows, just like a river flows, up and out of Girl's mouth. Us brothers, we float our made-out-of-mud boat down this made-out-of-mud river. We row-row-row our boat singing songs that float up from the bottom of our boots. Girl breathes a river is what us brothers sing as we dip our mud oars into this muddy water, this muddy river where, sometimes, in some places, it is so muddy that our paddles become shovels digging down into dirt. And this boat that is us brothers'? It is no longer a boat for us brothers to row in. What this boat becomes is, it becomes a tractor. And back behind us, in our mud-tailed rooster's tail of a wake, we spit out from our singing fish mouths songs that turn into seeds, then seedlings, that turn into full-grown trees: trees that rise up and leaf up from the bottom of this river's bottom: so many islands of so much green growing in the middle of so much water: so much water that looks so much like mud that it must be mud. And this, brother, are you picturing this? This muddy river that we are now floating down, that we are going down: it is a garden. It is ours for us brothers to keep.

Fish Heads: Revisited, or The Fish Head that Got Away

Once, us brothers, we caught us a fish with a fish head so big, us brothers, we couldn't cut off this fish's head. This fish, fished up and out from the dirty river that runs through this dirty river town, when we tried to cut off this fish's fish head, this fish, it would not die. Us brothers, with our fish-cutting knives fished up out of our trouser pockets, we couldn't cut through it, this fish, this fish's big head. We took turns, us brothers did, trying to cut off this fish's big fish head. We even worked us brothers together, cutting at this fish's head like brothers, one brother holding onto each end of the knife and each of us brothers sawing, back and forth, back and forth with this fish-cutting knife. Us brothers, we'd seen pictures of men with big men beards, lumberjacks with boots laced up to their knees, cutting down trees like this, working the big-toothed saw blade between them together, cutting down trees so big these men could actually stand up inside the cut that they were making to make a tree come falling down. Us brothers, we sawed like this, back and forth and back and forth, cutting and cutting, chopping and chopping, the knife's silvery blade singing between us, in our hands, until our hands began to bleed. But this big fish with its big fish head, this fish, it wouldn't die, its fish head, it wouldn't let us cut it off. Even when, us brothers, after a time, we took our knife and we stuck it, we stabbed it, straight down into the top of this fish's big fish head, even still, even then, this fish, it didn't stop its living. This fish, with this fish-cutting knife sticking up and out from the top of its big fish head, us brothers, we washed our hands of this big fish. Back to the river, us brothers, we hissed these words into the eyes of this fish, and like this, us brothers, we each of us stuck our arms, in up to our elbows, up and inside the big red gills of this big, big-headed fish. And like this, each of us brothers, each one of us standing by the sides of this fish, we dragged this fish back to the river. Go, Fish, we said to this fish. Be free, we said, and we pushed and we rolled this big, big-headed fish out into the river's muddy water. Like this, this fish, it swam away, it did not say to us brothers thank you or goodbye. But wait, us brothers, we called out to this fish after we'd just told it to go back away. Our knife! us brothers, we cried out after and out to this fish. You forgot to give us back our knife! Our knife, the knife that we used to cut off the heads off of our fish, this knife that we used to gut the guts out of our fish, it was still sticking up and out from the top of this fish's big fish head. This fish, with its fish head still on it, it didn't listen to us brothers. To this fish, us brothers, we could not say to it, Good, Fish. Us brothers, we stood there like this, on the muddy edge of this dirty river that runs its way through this dirty river town, and we watched this fish, out and into our river, this fish, it swam itself away. After a while, us brothers, the only part of this fish that we could see was the sticking-up knife, sticking up out of this fish's big fish head, cutting through the mud that was the river. And then, after a little while more, there was no more knife left for us brothers to see, there was only the river with this fish somewhere down inside it, there was only the moon in the sky and the mud of the river holding us all in this place.

The Moon is a Fish

One night, us brothers, we lifted up our fishing knives up to the moon and we sliced it open, we gutted it, the moon, just like we would a fish. Yes, the moon, it was a fish, floating up above us brothers in that rivery dark, and out of the moon's big white beautiful belly buckets of fish guts came rivering out. Us brothers, we were up to our boy necks in fish guts and more fish guts. The river, too, it was a river of fish guts and rivering fish guts. Up out of this river of river and guts it was Girl who came walking up to us brothers, to see what it was us brothers were up to and doing, with our boy heads just barely sticking up out of all of these guts. The moon, us brothers, we lifted up our heads up to say these words to Girl: the moon, we told this to Girl, it is a fish. Girl looked up. She looked up to the sky, at the moon up in the sky, and then she looked back down at us brothers: us brothers just a couple of sticking up brothers sticking up from the river's mud and the moon's fish-gut heads. You can't gut the moon, Girl said. She shook her girl head. The moon, it's not yours for you brothers to keep. When Girl looked with her made-out-of-mud eyes down upon us brothers, we could see that her eyes, they were not their usual muddy moons. Girl's eyes, the look looking out from the insides of them, us brothers, we could feel the sun inside of them burning out. It was Brother's idea, Brother looked at me and said. Brother was the brother of us brothers, Brother said to Girl, who made us do what it was that we did. I looked at Brother then. There was this look that us brothers sometimes liked to look at each other with. It was the kind of a look that actually hurt the eyes of the brother who was doing the looking. Imagine that look. Look: I took back that look. I did not shake my head at Brother. I did not say to Girl that Brother was the brother of us who was making all of this up. Girl just stood there, for a while, above us brothers, and then, after a little while more, she reached down toward us brothers with her muddy girl hand. I'm only going to ask you this once, Girl said to us brothers then. Which one of you brothers did it? Girl said. Which one of you boys raised up your knife to make the moon into a fish? I looked up at Girl. I looked back over at Brother. I waited to see what was about to happen to us brothers next. It was a long few seconds. The sky above the river, the sky above the steel mill—it sitting shipwrecked there in the riverbank's mud—it was dark and it was quiet. Somewhere, I knew, the sun was shining. I nodded. I knew right then what it was that I had to do. We were brothers. So I was the brother of us brothers who lifted his hand up. It was me, I said this with my mouth. I was the brother, I said this to Girl, who turned the moon into a fish. I am the brother of us who made this fish-gutted mess. Girl looked down at us brothers and she ran her girl fingers through her made-out-of-mud girl hair. You give me no choice here was what Girl said to us brothers next. Up at Girl, I nodded my boy head. Then I closed both of my eyes. I did not see it, but I knew what it was that she was doing, when Girl reached down with her hand and took the knife from out of my hand. I could hear her take it, this knife, with mud and more mud and fish guts dripping off it, and she ran it, dragged it, Girl wiped it, onto her girl leg. Then Girl raised it up, into the sky above us brothers, into the sky above the river, and she chopped off Brother's head.

The Dead Man's Boat

There are, in this dirty river town, with this dirty river running through it, fishering men and fishering women who like to fish from boats. But us brothers, unlike all of them, we do our fishing standing on the river's muddy shore. These boats that we see, out on the river, with these fishering people standing up inside them, we see them all day long going up and down the river looking for fish. Sometimes we see these boats and it looks like to us brothers that they are, all of the time, just running up and down the river *looking* for fish and not ever doing any actual fishing. Us brothers, we could never get it into our heads why a fishering man or fishering woman would need a boat for them to fish with. We always figured let the fish come to us. Which is what the fish usually did. But there was a time, one summer, when it seemed like to us brothers that the fish in our river had gone off to be fish in some other river other than ours. Us brothers, we couldn't imagine a river other than ours. We couldn't picture a fish that would want to be a fish in some other river other than *our* river. Our river was a dirty river, it was a good river, us brothers believed, for dirty river fish like ours to be fish in. Us brothers, we loved this dirty river town with this dirty river running through it where we could always run down to it to fish. But there was that summer. That summer, those dirty river fish of ours that we always used to fish from out of this dirty river that runs its way through this dirty river town, it was as if these fish had gone away to be fish in some other dirty river town other than ours. How could they? was what us brothers wanted to know. We didn't want to believe that our fish might be that kind of fish. In the end, about all this, it was wrong for us brothers to think this about these fish. Our fish, they hadn't left our dirty river, our dirty river town. What happened to our fish was this. It was hot, that summer, and the sky, that summer, it never seemed to turn gray with the promise of rain. A river, us brothers, we soon discovered, it needs rain for it to be a river. Just like a fish needs a river for it to be a fish. By midsummer, that summer, when us brothers made our way down to the dirty river where we always ran ourselves down to its muddy banks to fish for our dirty river fish, there was more mud, down there, that summer, than there was river down there. It looked like to us brothers, to our boy eyes, that the river, too, just like our fish, like it too had gone, it was going, away. The river, it was true, it had gotten thinner along its usual muddy banks. And along the banks of this dirty river, there was more dirt, that summer, than there was mud made by the river's water. But the river, us brothers, we believed in this, deep in our muddy brother hearts, it would always be the river to us. No one or no thing could take the river away from us. And the fish, too, us brothers, we believed this: the fish were somewhere out in the river too. Where the fish were, that summer, out in the river, us brothers, we couldn't get ourselves out to. The fish, we found this out, the fish were out in the river's channels, and out farther too out where the river turns east to become the lake. To the river's channels and out into the lake was where our fish had gone off too: not to some other river, but to this other place in the river and out in that other place too—the lake—that the river flowed out to, though both of these places, us brothers, we could not get out to, not without a boat. Us brothers, we didn't have us brothers a boat for us to go out fishing for these fish in, out where the fish were out there in the river's deeper down waters, out where the river's bottom was deeper down, down there in the river where there was more river for the fish to be fish in. We need us a boat, Brother one night, that summer, he pointed this out. Brother was the brother of us brothers who was always saying what the both of us brothers already were thinking. Brother was that kind of a brother. We'd been for the past few nights the both of us brothers both of us thinking this thought, though this was the first time one of us said it out loud outside our own boy heads. It was at night when Brother said what he said about us brothers needing us a boat. Up in the sky, that night, the moon was, as it always seemed to be for us brothers, big and shining white. The river, in the moon's light, it was laid out for us brothers like a silver shimmering fish. Us brothers, we needed us a boat. You can say that again was what I said to Brother. And when I said what I said, when I said these words to Brother, that's when it happened. Out there in the river's moonlit night, out there out on the river, there in the river's dark, out of the corners of us brothers' eyes, we saw it: a boat. There was a boat out there out on the river slowly floating down the river. This was a boat floating slowly down the river without any lights on it to light the river's way. Us brothers, we ran ourselves down to the river to see who it was who was out on this boat, to see who it was who was out on the river, at night, in a boat without any lights. But us brothers, even though the moon was big and white, we couldn't see anyone, no fishering man or fishering woman, standing up or sitting down on the inside of this boat. We even called out to it, this boat, Hey, your lights! Both of us brothers hollered out, Turn on your lights! But only the rivery echoes of our own boy voices returned to us from the river's dark. So what us brothers did then was this. We walked out, into the river, across the river's sparkling dark, out to where this dark boat was darkly drifting, out to where this boat without any lights on it was floating down the river on the river's downriver flow. Careful, Brother, Brother said, as the river crept up around our necks, our heads floating, or looking like they were floating, like a couple of chopped off fish heads. Don't drown, Brother said. When Brother said what was in his boy head, I turned to face Brother in his face. Half of his brother face was lit up in the moon's lighthouse light. What I said to Brother then was this: Fish don't drown, Brother, I said. To a fish the river is its home. When I said this to Brother, Brother gave me this look. There was this look that us brothers we sometimes liked to look at each other with this look. It was the kind of a look that actually hurt the eyes of the brother who was doing the looking. Imagine that look. Brother's mouth opened up wide like a fish drinking in water. Let's keep on walking then, Brother said to this. And so, us brothers, out into the muddy river, out across the river's water, we walked, and walked, and kept on walking, walking through muddy water, walking out to where this boat, it was floating and floating away. When the river reached up above our boy eyes, above our fishy heads, that's when the both of us brothers took in a deep breath. Like this, like fish, us brothers, with the river's muddy water covering us brothers up, us brothers, our mouths opening up, like this we began to breathe.

The Dead Man's Boat: Revisited

We are down by the river, fishing for fish, when we see what it is that we see. What we see is there is a man, walking across the muddy river's muddy water, this man, he is walking right up to us brothers. Boys, this man says. Brothers, he adds. I'm looking for my boat. Have you seen it, my boat? is what this man with his man's mouth says. This man, his mouth, it is a hole in his face with a fish sticking its fish head out of it. When he sees us looking at him like this, like he is a man with a fish sticking out of his mouth, he spits this fish out into the river. This fish, when it hits the river, into the river it swims away. We see lots of boats is what us brothers say next to this man. There are lots of boats running up and down up and down this river with people inside them fishing for the river's fish. But us brothers, we say to this man, we do our fishing standing right here on the river's muddy shore. Us brothers don't need us a boat. Must be lots of fish in this river if there's lots of boats fishing this river for fish is what this man says to this. It wouldn't be a river without the fish that make the river what it is, is what us brothers say then to this. Brother adds, What's your boat look like? That might help us to tell you if we think we've seen it. If one of you brothers stood on the other brother's shoulders, you'd need two more brothers of you to be as big as my boat is big, this man says. That's big, Brother says to this. It's big enough is what this man says then to this. What else? Brother asks. What else do we need to know? My boat, this man tells us, it's made out of steel. Steel, us brothers say. A boat made out of steel? Us brothers, we give each other this look. There is this look that us brothers sometimes like to look at each other with. It's the kind of a look that actually hurts the eyes of the brother who is doing the looking. Imagine that look. Maybe, we say, to this man, it sank, we say, to this man. This man, when we say this to this man, he looks down at us brothers with eyes that are made out of steel. What makes you say that? is what this man says to us brothers then, looking at us with this cold steel look looking out from his cold steel eyes. Steel sinks is what us brothers say to this. Like stones, we tell him, and we reach down to the river's muddy bank and pick up from the mud into our boy fists two fist-sized stones that we throw out into the river. Both of these stones, when they hit the river's muddy water, these stones turn into fish. Us brothers, we don't say anything to this man about this. What we do say, though, is this. Mister, we say. Maybe you should look with your look beginning at the bottom of the river. Start looking there is what we tell him. This man, he looks the look in his cold steel eyes down upon us brothers, us standing down by this muddy river's muddy shore, then he looks his look up into the sky above the river where the sun is somewhere shining. This man, he is nodding with his man head as he searches the above-the-river sky, looking there, into the clouds, so it looks like to us, for his boat made out of steel, then he turns and walks out into the river from which, he just a little while ago, came walking out across it, like a stone that somebody skipped. The river, this time, it does not hold this walking man up. The river, this time, it is a fish's big fish mouth opening up and swallowing down inside of it a fish as small as a man's last breath.

The Dead Man's Boat: Revisited

Us brothers, we took us our mud and our fish-fishing poles baited with worms and rust and mud and we hopped up into the dead man's boat, that boat that we found washed up on our dirty river's dirty shores, and we headed ourselves upriver, up past the shipwrecked mill where our father used to go inside to work, it sitting dark and silenced and fireless there on the river's muddy bank, up around the bend in the river, past the other string of mills farther north along the river, mills with fires still burning there inside them, up toward where the beaded lights of that big steel bridge stretching from our side of the river all the way over to the river's other side, it was all lit up in the night like a constellation of sunken-ship stars, each star shining out in the nighttime's dark like the shiny heads of nails hammered into some backyard pole. We were chugging along, us brothers, with Brother sitting up in the bow, holding up a lantern's light for us to better see the river by, and the brother that I am was kneeling in the back of the boat, what's called the stern, with one hand on the outboard's tiller, the other hand hanging itself over the edge of the boat, the fingers of that hand dragging themselves across the muddy skin of the river. We were on our way upriver, up to the where the dirty river that runs through our dirty river town, it runs all the way up through the city, us brothers heading up there to see if we might catch us some of the big city's big dirty river fish, when out of nowhere in the night and in the river's muddy dark we heard, then saw, a boat, much bigger than ours, it was cutting across and down the river, it was heading right for us brothers. There's a boat coming right for us, Brother turned his head and said as he held up the lantern light with that fire glowing inside it so that his face flashed full like the moon. I looked up at Brother then. There was a look that us brothers sometimes liked to look at each other with. It was the kind of a look that actually hurt the eyes of the brother who was doing the looking. Imagine that look. Do I look like a brother born blind? was what I said to Brother then, and I cut the tiller hard and to the right. But that boat, that other boat much bigger than ours, that boat with us brothers not sitting down inside it, it kept on coming toward us brothers, as if it didn't see us brothers, as if us brothers weren't even there. But it saw us, this boat, the people sitting there inside it: this, us brothers, we knew. When we moved it, our boat, it moved closer toward where it was we moved. And before we knew what next to do, because we knew we couldn't outrun it, this boat, it was soon coming across our bow, it was doing what it could do to hit us, this boat, even though we didn't, we couldn't, know why. What did we, us brothers, do, to a boat like this boat? Us brothers, all we ever really did out on the river was fish. We didn't know what we should do, us brothers, other than what we ended up doing. Us brothers, the both of us brothers, we both jumped, heads first, out of our boat, the dead man's boat, the dead man who fell into the river pissing into the river for luck, we headed ourselves, down into the river, and we swam ourselves down to get us away from this coming-after-us boat. When we stuck up our boy heads up out of the river, to see if we were both of us still alive, to see where our boat was, to see where that other boat was, all us brothers could see was our boat drifting its way back and down the river, back to from where us brothers, ourselves, had just come from. That other boat, it seemed, had all but disappeared, and not even the sound of it could be heard by our ears. Our boat, the dead man's boat, away from us brothers, it had drifted too far away from us brothers for us to be able to swim back to it for us to get back in it. So, us brothers, we swam ourselves toward the river's muddy shore, we swam ourselves out of us brothers' breath, and plopped ourselves down in the mud at the edge of the river. Yes, like a couple of out-of-water fish, us brothers, there in the mud, we sucked in at the air until the sky above us, it helped us brothers to begin breathing. We stood up, in the mud, out of the mud, but we did not wipe the mud off us. Us brothers, we liked mud and the fishy river smells that always smelled of river and mud and fish. With mud in our eyes, us brothers, we turned to look one last time back downriver, to where our boat, the dead man's boat, it had floated downriver and down around a bend in the river and almost out of sight, this boat with our fishing poles inside it, our buckets empty of fish. Us brothers, we didn't know what we were going to do, or how we were going to get back home, now that we didn't have us brothers a boat to take us back home in. So what us brothers did was, we figured it, in our boy heads, that it was too early in the night for us to head ourselves back home. We'd gone out, that night, out onto the river, out on the river in the dead man's boat, to spend the dark night fishing. It was what us brothers did, at night, and in the morning, and sometimes, too, in the day: we fished. Our mother and our father both believed that we were brothers sound asleep in our beds when we stepped outside through our bedroom's window and slipped, as we always did, down to the river. We had until the sun's rise for us brothers to get us back home before our father would call out to us to wake us with the word, Son. When our father called out to us brothers, Son, we both knew, we were crossing that dirty river together. But us brothers, we didn't want to go back home, to bed, in a room in a house with our mother and father asleep in it. Our house, with our mother and father in it, it was not the kind of a house that us brothers liked to go back to. The river, out fishing on the river, that was where us brothers liked to be. But now, us brothers, we didn't have us brothers a boat to be out on the river in, we didn't have us our fish-fishing poles for us to fish for our fish with, we didn't have us our buckets of mud and rust and worms for us brothers to bait our hooks with. It was just us brothers now standing on the upriver banks of a river and a city that was not ours. Our mother and our father both had often told us brothers that the city was not a place for us boys to be. Don't ever go, was what our mother told us. But us brothers, we didn't much like to listen to what our mother liked to tell us. Our mother, she was the kind of a mother who told us brothers not to walk through mud, a mother who told us to wash our hands before we ate, our hands that always smelled of fish, our hands with mud dried hard in our palms. We liked mud and we liked it the way the fish's fishy silver scales stuck to our hands. These were fish that we fished out of the dirty river that runs its way through this dirty river town, fish that we took these fish back home with us and we gutted the guts out of those fish, we cut off the heads off of those fish, and then we hammered them, those fish, those fish heads, into the backyard telephone pole out back in the back of our yard. In the end, there was exactly a hundred and fifty fish heads, hammered and nailed into that pole's creosoted wood. Each fish, each fish head, us brothers, we gave each one a name. Not one was called Jimmy or John. Jimmy and John was mine and my brother's name. We called each other Brother. Brother, Brother said to me then. What do you want to do? Brother was the brother of us brothers who always liked to ask these kinds of questions. To Brother, I did not know what then to say. Us brothers, we stood there like that on the dirty river's dirty banks, and we looked around this place that us brothers, we'd been told, this was not the kind of a place for us brothers to be. But this place, this city with this dirty river running through it, it didn't look much different than the town that was ours with its dirty river running through it and with its dirty river mill built up along its dirty river banks, its smokestacks that stained the sky the color of rust and mud. We liked a sky that was stained the color of rust and mud. Our mother once let it be known to us brothers that there was a sky, there was a sky, our mother told us, bigger than the sky above the river that was ours. Us brothers, we couldn't picture this, a sky bigger than the sky that was our backyard. We couldn't picture a town without a dirty river running through it where us brothers could run down to it to fish. This is our river, was what we said to our mother then, and this was what I said to Brother too. This is our river, I said, then. There's no place else for us to be. We stood there, like this, for a while, like this, just standing there along the edge of the river. The moon in the sky had not yet begun to rise. The sky, it was mostly dark. Behind us, away from the river, most of the houses sitting side by side in the dark, these houses did not have lights lighting them up from inside them. We stood there, on the edge of this river, but us brothers, we couldn't fish. We reached down into the mud and found us some stones and we threw them out and into the river. Sometimes the stones skipped. Sometimes, in the dark, the stones made a sound like a fish leaping up out of the water. Us brothers, we knew more about fish than most people know about fish. Us brothers know that when a fish jumps up out of the water, what that means is that that fish, it isn't a fish for us brothers to fish for and catch: not with our fishing hooks baited thick with mud and sunk down to the river's bottom. Us brothers, we didn't know how to fish for fish that were fish that jumped up as if to bite the sky. It's true, sometimes us brothers, we could walk out into the river and reach with our hands down into the river and fish us up some fish with our bare boy hands. It's true, too, that we could sometimes dunk our buckets into the river and like this we'd fill up our buckets with a mix of fish and mud. But it was not one of those kinds of nights for us brothers. Us brothers, we didn't have us our buckets or our poles or a boat for us to fish from. And our hands, us brothers, hanging down by our legs, they were all four of them balled up into fists. Let's go for a walk, was what I said to Brother then, and we both of us turned and started walking in from the river, up past houses that did not look like anyone was living inside them. There were no lights lit up and burning on the insides of these houses, there were no streetlights lighting up the streets outside. But us brothers, we had us eyes like the marbly eyes of fish, eyes that, like moons, could see in the river at night. And so, us brothers, into this dark, we walked. We walked and we walked, it didn't matter where, until the mud on our boots had all of the way been walked off. That's how us brothers liked to wash the mud from off the bottoms of our boots. We didn't like it when our mother made us wash the mud off with a brush held in our hands. So we walked, and we walked, but we did not see a face that looked like the faces that were ours. It was as if, us brothers, we had walked into a dead town, or maybe it was just a town that was early to bed asleep. Even the stars in the sky above this dead town seemed not to be shining. But still, us brothers, we walked. We did not talk. We just listened to the voice that was us brothers inside the each of our boy heads. In this town, even the cars that we saw, here on our walk, they all of them seemed to be made out of rust. What us brothers needed was a couple of fishing poles for us to do some fishing with. Even though the fish were jumping, this night, maybe us brothers could get those fish to go back down to the river's muddy bottom. So we went looking around town for two poles for us to fish with. There was a store with a sign above the door that said on it, Del Ray's Live Bait, but the door, when we pulled on it to get it to open, it did not open up. There were other buildings with the same two words on it, Del Ray, Del Ray, some of them, these words, spraypainted on pieces of wood nailed into brick, DEL RAY, DEL RAY, but these doors, too, to these other buildings, they wouldn't open up for us either. So what us brothers did then was, we turned back around and we decided in our heads to head ourselves back downriver. If we started walking along the road that runs its way along the banks of the river, we'd get home before the night began its turning into day. Us brothers, we were walking back this way, back downriver, back toward where we lived in a house with a mother and father inside it, when Brother turned and said that he was tired of all this walking. Would you rather swim back home? was what I said to Brother. Brother said what we both knew, it was too cold for us to be all the way back home in the river swimming. What we need, Brother said, is another boat, Brother said. I looked at Brother. I nodded with my head at what Brother said. Brother was right. Us brothers, we did need us a boat. It didn't have to be a fancy boat. The dead man's boat, it wasn't a fancy boat. It was a boat that floats is all that it was, a boat that we found washed up on the river's dirty river banks one day when the man that it once belonged to had fallen and drowned when he pissed into the river for luck. What other kind of a boat did brothers like us need? So we started looking with our eyes into the backyards of these unlit houses to see if we could find us a boat to get us brothers back on the river on. But in the backyards of these houses, houses not far from the banks of the river that runs itself down and through our dirty river town, there were cars rusting in the backyards of these houses—cars with no wheels and cars with the windows in them busted out and cars with weeds as tall as us brothers growing up on all sides of these cars so that the cars were hard for us brothers to see. But boats: there were no boats to be seen in these backyards for us brothers to see: no boats for us brothers to get back out on the river on, to take us brothers back home. Us brothers, we were standing out on the corner of Jefferson, that road that runs along the river, all the way from the big dirty city back to our dirty river town, when out of the dark, us brothers, we could see what we knew it, it was the shadow of a man coming on toward us. This man, this shadow, who here in the near river dark did not seem to have a face that us brothers could see it, he walked right up to us brothers, as if he knew us, and asked us what were we looking for. Who says we're looking for something was what Brother's mouth opened itself up to say. When Brother said this to this shadow of a man, this man without a face, I shot Brother this look. There was this look that us brothers sometimes liked to look at each other with. It was the kind of a look that actually hurt the eyes of the brother who was doing the looking. Imagine that look. When this man didn't say anything to this, I stepped in front of Brother and said that it's true, we were looking for something. A boat was what I said into this man's shadowy face. This man, when I said this to his face, the look on his face seemed to lighten. It was like a light winced on when I said the word boat. Then he turned his face away from us brothers and he started walking down along the river. Come, this man said. Stay close. Us brothers, we did what we'd been told. It's true that, us brothers, we'd been told, by our mother and father, like most boys have been told: don't talk to strangers, don't talk with your mouth full, don't walk into the house with mud on the bottoms of your boots. But us brothers, we weren't the kind of boys who liked to listen to this sort of talk. When we heard our mother say the word don't, us brothers, what we did was, we did. And so, us brothers, we walked in the shadows of this shadowy man, this man whose face was more shadow than it was flesh or even fish. We walked down along the river, past bars with steel bars rusted on the boarded up windows, past more buildings with the words DEL RAY written on their sides. After a while, we found ourselves standing outside the fenced-in yard of a hardware store, its backyard filled with boats. It was a boatyard of boats, this backyard was, and it was, to our eyes, like finding a river in the desert for us to make mud with. Us brothers, with our eyes, we looked and we looked at all of those boats. There were boats made out of steel and boats made of aluminum and boats that were made out of wood. Us brothers, we liked boats made out of wood best because it was hard for us to figure out how a thing made out of steel could float. What, we wondered, kept it from down-to-the-river's-bottom sinking? This was something that us brothers, we hadn't yet learned the reason why. So, the man turned and turned his shadow face to ours, which boat would you boys like? There was a wood boat there that looked like it had been painted with mud. Us brothers, we both looked at each other and knew that that boat was made for us. We pointed with our hands toward this mud-colored boat. The man who was more shadow than flesh or fish, he pointed with his hand, he pushed at this fence, and the gate of it swung away from its rusted lock. You boys sure you want that boat, the man asked. You could have any boat here. He waved at them all with his hand as if to say that they were us brothers' boats to take. It doesn't have a motor on its back, the man pointed this out. We're sure, we said, and nodded our boy heads. We don't need us a motor for us to get us back home, we said. The river will take us where we need to go, we said. Then it's yours, the man said. I'll even help you walk it down to the river. And this, we did. Us brothers, we lifted this boat made out of wood, this boat the color of mud, this boat that almost looked like it might be made out of mud, we held up its back, and the man who was a shadow to us brothers, he lifted this boat up by its front. And then we walked it, like this, this boat, down to the river, down to where the river's edge was a mix of mud and stones and broken slabs of concrete. We set the boat down, there at the river's muddy-watered edge, and got in. The man with the dark face dug his heels into the mud and pushed us brothers off and out into the river's dark. We paddled with our hands out into the river's swirling current. It was a good current. It wouldn't be long before we drifted ourselves back and to our town. Us brothers, we raised our hands above our boy heads to say to this man goodbye. Thank you we said with our mouths, but only the river heard this. This man, at us brothers floating away, he raised up his hand at us too. He was a good man, us brothers, we knew. This man, like us brothers did too, he knew a good boat when he saw it. The moon in the sky was now rising up out of the river. This moon, it threw down its rope of moony light, but still, that man's face, it was a face that us brothers, we could not see it. We could not see any eyes on that man's shadowy face. We could not see a mouth. His mouth was just a hole in his face that sounds sometimes came out of that place. Somewhere in there there must have been a tongue, us brothers figured. Unless this man was the father of Boy, that boy, who was a brother to nobody, born with a full head of hair but with no tongue on the inside of his mouth. We're going home was what I said to Brother then, and I turned to look at him in his face. Brother's face, it was a face like mine, a face with a nose and two eyes and a mouth and a chin that sometimes had mud dried on it. It won't be long now, Brother nodded and said. Tomorrow, I said, will be a new day for us, Brother, with a new boat for us brothers to fish from. For this, we had that man, whose face we could not see, whose name we did not ask for or know, to thank. Us brothers, we turned one last time back upriver to wave at this man our thanks. In the moon's rivery light, we could see him walking, this man, out into the river, out onto the river, and the river, it was holding him, this man, up. He did not see us, this man, as he walked and he kept on walking on, he did not turn to look our way, until he had walked himself all the way across the river to the river's other side, walking and walking and walking on until there was nothing left on the river for us brothers to see, there was nothing left for us brothers to hear, only the sound that the river sometimes makes when a stone is skipped across it.

The Hole at the Bottom of the River

There was a part of the river, a piece of the river, a hole in the river, there was a hole down there that reached down so deep that no body, no fishing man or fishing woman, had ever touched its bottom: no anchor, no barbed fishing hook, no cast-iron sinker, which is to say that nothing that had gone down searching into the river in search of that bottomless place had ever found what it had gone down there looking for. It's true that this was a part of the river that even us brothers, us muddy river boys, did not with our muddy eyes ever get a chance to see. We had imagined that place: we had imagined it to be deep and dark and muddy, just the kind of a place where us brothers could feel at home at. We wanted to get down to it. We wanted to touch this place with our boy hands. We just knew it in our boy heads that there had to be some way for us brothers to get down to it: it was just that no body, no fishering man or fishering woman, no fish-fishing boy or girl had figured out how to do it. Until now. Until it was going to be us brothers who were the ones to figure how out: figure out how to get down to it. So what us brothers did was this: we rounded up all the rope we could get our hands around—ropes that our mother used to use to hang our no longer muddy clothes up on, ropes used by tugboat and fishing boat men to anchor down their boats. We even stole a roll of coiled-up steel wire that was used to carry our town's power from house to house. And we knotted them all up together to make for us brothers one big long rope: a rope so long that if one of us brothers were to hold onto one end of it and the other one of us were to take the other end of it and walk off with it into another direction, the brother who was doing the walking might as well never picture himself ever coming to a rest. Or see it like this: if the world was flat, an open hand held out to the sky—and let me tell you, I'm not so sure that it's not, that is, that it isn't flat—that walking with the rope brother would walk right off the edge of that held-out hand before he would feel the tug of no more rope left to walk with. Get the picture? So with this rope in hand, us brothers, we walked off down to the river's muddy shore, down to where we unstuck from the mud where it was sitting a flat-bottom fishing boat, its metal flaking with rust, and us brothers, we straddled ourselves aboard and shoved off with it out into the river. It was us brothers with Girl saddled in between us, there in the boat's middle, so that the boat, with the all of us sitting inside it, it would not tip with us sitting us like this. So like this, picture this, we oared our way out to where we knew this was where the river's bottom was a bottomy hole down at the river's bottom. When we dropped our anchor over the side of the boat and when it did not bite into any bottom, us brothers, we knew that this was where we wanted to be. Here, then, us brothers, we made us a loop in the rope and we looped it over the top of Girl: we knotted it tight, but not too tight, up around Girl's belly. Girl's belly button, let me tell you this, it is a hole with its own story to tell, but tell it, I won't, not right now. And so with a tug, a hug, and a kiss from each of us brothers—goodbye, Girl, good luck, we'll see you when you get back up—we watched Girl jump into the river. Into the river we watched Girl sink. Like this, Girl disappeared from us brothers. But us brothers, we held onto Girl tight, we held onto our lives, we held on tight to the tied-together line that was singing in our hands. This line, it sang through our boy fingers. This rope, it ran, and then it kept on running, it kept on going: a rope made out of song, a rope made out of water, rope made out of mud and sand. Us brothers, we did not know what the sounds being sung by this rope meant for us brothers, or what they meant for Girl. But still, we held on to that singing song singing as the rope ran through our holding on hands. Back at the river's edge, the wake that Girl made when she dove headfirst into the river, it rocked a handful of the houses built right on the river right off of their stone block housings. Us brothers, we watched these on-the-river houses float on down, down the river, and were then gone down the river, they went a-bobbing away out toward the lake. We did not raise our hands to wave goodbye to our in-bed, in-our-house mother. Our hands were too filled with song. It burned our boy hands, our ears were on fire. It'd be years before this singing, for us brothers, stopped. Us brothers, we kept on holding on to that song. We held on and did not get any older. When this singing finally did stop—how many years or centuries later was it?—we waited for Girl to give us brothers both a tug, to say to us brothers that she had gotten down to the river's bottom, down to that dark and rivery hole: tug twice to tell us brothers to pull Girl back up from the river's bottom back up. After ten years, we got tug number one. After ten years more, or maybe it was ten-hundred years later, two other tugs put us brothers to the task of pulling Girl back up, back up to this other world where, us brothers, we were here patiently waiting. Hand after hand, hand over hand, us brothers, we pulled Girl up. It took us brothers ten years more to get Girl back up to us brothers. Girl, she was that far down inside the river's hole. When we did get Girl back, when we asked her, so what was down there at the river's bottom, down where no body had ever gone down there to see, Girl told us that she saw, down there, a man who looked a lot like us brothers sometimes looked, only this man, Girl told us, he was bigger and he was older than us, with whiskers on his man face where us brothers only had just fuzz. He said, she said, that this man was a man who called himself God. And what did Girl and this man who called himself God do for all of those down-in-the-river years? He wanted, he tried, to kiss me, Girl told us. And what did Girl do to God wanting from Girl a kiss? Us brothers, we held our breath. We waited to hear what Girl was going to say. It was a long few seconds. The sky above the river, the sky above the river where the steel mill was shipwrecked in the mud, it was dark and quiet. Somewhere, I was sure, the sun was shining. I did what I had to do, was what Girl said. And what was that? Tell us, us brothers said. What did you do? I did, Girl said, what I'd do to any boy or man or brother who tried to kiss me without asking. And what did Girl do? Is this what you, too, are wondering with us now? Well, let us tell you. What Girl said, what Girl did was, are you listening to this? Are you ready for this? Are your ears ready to hear? Girl bit off God's whole head.

Our Mother is a Fish

One night, us brothers, we go to get our mother by the elbows up, up out of her sleeping bed, and we walk her back into our back of the house room, and here we lay her body down into the bed that, us brothers, this is where we do our sleeping in. Go to sleep, we say, to this mother of ours. Rest up. But when we lay our mother's body down into this bed that is our brothers', this bed, it is not a big enough bed for our mother's body to fit all the way down in it. Our mother's legs, when we lay her head down like this in this not-big-enough bed, her mother legs stick out from this bed's bottom, what our mother always calls the bed's foot. And when, us brothers, we push down hard with our boy hands to get our mother's legs to go back up into us brothers' bed, the head that is our mother's, it sticks up and out from the head that is the bed's top. Us brothers, we go back and forth like this, pushing the head that is our mother's back into where the bed and the pillow is, then it's us pushing our mother's legs and feet back up so that they don't hang down off of where the foot of this bed is: head, legs, push, head, legs, push: get the picture? We walk around and around this bed that is us brothers' and we look all around this room to see if there is some way for us to get our mother's whole body, her head and her legs and feet, to get all of this to fit into this bed that is us brothers' bed for us to share. Us brothers, we don't know what we are going to do, or how we are going to get our mother—her head, her legs, her feet—into our bed, until we look outside our bedroom's window and there we see our fish. Outside our bedroom's window, out back in the back of our house's backyard, us brothers, there is a back-of-the-yard telephone pole studded with the chopped off heads of fish. These fish, these fishes' fish heads, hammered and nailed into this pole's creosoted wood, they are looking back out at us brothers, open-eyed, open-mouthed, and it's like they're singing to us brothers. When, us brothers, we see these fishes, these fish heads, singing out to us brothers like this, us brothers, we know that there is only one thing that us brothers can do. Brother, I say to Brother, and I nod at him with my head. You can go first. Brother, I say, give me your hand, I say. Hold your hand out against this room's dark. Brother, being the brother that he is, Brother does what he is told. Good, Brother, I say. We are brothers, us brothers are. We are each other's voices inside our own heads. Here, I take hold of Brother's hand like this, and then I hand to him, into Brother's reached out hand, the knife that, us brothers, we use this knife to gut out the guts and to cut off the heads off of the fish that we fish out of this dirty river that runs its way through this dirty river town. Mother, Brother says, and here, us brothers, we look at each other with our look. There is this look that us brothers, we sometimes like to look at each other with this look. It's the kind of a look that actually hurts the eyes of the brother who is doing the looking. Imagine that look. This is gonna hurt you, Brother says to our mother, more than it is going to hurt us, Brother says. And just like this, us brothers, with one brother's hand teaching the other, we take hold of our mother like this, and like this, and like this. Like this, we cut off our mother's head.

Our Father in the Belly of the Fish

Us brothers, we go down to the river to look for our walking-out father. Our father, us brothers, we believe this, he is down by the river, he is down here, a part of us believes, at the bottom of the muddy river. When we call out to our father his name, when that word father comes floating up and out from out of our open boy mouths, we are fearing that the sound that our mouths make, those burbly sounds bumping up against all of this muddy river water, we are afraid, us brothers are, that these sounds that we are making, our hunting hollerings out of, father, where are you, father? father, come out, come out, wherever you are: we are afraid, us brothers are, that these words that are ours are going, that they have gone, by our father, by our father's ears, unheard. And so, what we do is, instead of us keeping on with this calling out to our father our father's name and having that word make nothing but some muddy sound that not even the fish can make out what it is that us brothers are trying to say, we get it into our boy heads to start to look and to call out to our father the way we have heard it said that deaf people, those of our world who can't with their mouths make the sounds that are words, who can't with their ears hear the sounds that words make—yes, we have heard it said, yes, us brothers, we have seen it said too, that these people who are not like us, who don't talk like us, who don't hear like us, but they can, yes, they can and they do talk with their fingers: they make words come to life with their fingering hands. You have got to see it, if you haven't seen it, how beautiful it is to see these people speak without making a sound. How beautiful it is, it must be so beautiful, to be able to make words out of fingers that are made, by a twist of the wrist, by the bend of knuckles— these fingers that are made to look like to us brothers, they turn into letters, sentences made up of silent words, an alphabet made out of bone. And so, us brothers, we take up our bonied boy fingers, we make with our mud-dusty hands, shapes that we hope can do, here at the river, here at the bottom of this river that is ours, what our mouths seem unable to say when they try to mouth out that word, father. Look here. See how Brother, with his hand, he is closing it right now to make it into a fist. Hit is what this fist of his is saying. Or else: back off. Or, maybe yes: Brother I am ready to take it. My hand, this hand of mine that I say hello with this hand, with a wave of this hand that is mine, this hand that I pick up stones with and send them skipping across the muddy skin of this river that runs its way through this dirty river town: this hand that I hold the hammer with is what I am really wanting you to see: see this, it is the hand that I open it up so that the fingers on this hand are all five of them finning and fanning out. See my hand, see with my hand: it is a starfish that has risen up from the bottom of some long-ago rivery sea. This hand, it is a star calling out to our father his name. Us brothers, we each of us take turns fingering that word father so that our father might see it, so that he might rise up toward, a river-bottom fish swimming up toward the light of the moon: a fish leaping up, breaking through the sky of the river, opening up its fish mouth to take a bite of the moon. Father. We say this word with our hands held up for our father to see, to eat. We say this word father ten thousand times with our bony boy hands, our fingers gnawed down to the muddy nubs. We walk up and down the river's bottom but our father does not hear or see us. Only other fish swim up near to us brothers and come up to us brothers' calling out. The littler fish swim up to us brothers and nibble us on our fingers and toes. It is possible that they believe us to be their mothers. But the bigger fish, they swim up to us brothers and take our whole hands up inside their fish mouths. There is this one big fish that is the biggest big fish out of all of these coming up to us brothers fish. This fish, it is the biggest fish that the eyes of us brothers have ever before seen. This fish, it is as big as us brothers are big. If this big fish stood up on its big fish tail, this big fish, it might even be bigger than the both of us. I can see that Brother can see this too, so I look at Brother with this look. Us brothers, there is this look that we sometimes like to look at each other with. It is the kind of a look that actually hurts the eyes of the brother who is doing the looking. Imagine that look. Look now at us brothers. We are still looking at each other with this look that we sometimes look between us when we hear some rivery voice say, Boys, look inside. Look inside where? is what I am thinking, and because Brother is my brother, Brother says, out loud, these words that I am thinking. This big fish that is bigger than the both of us, it is then that this fish, it opens up its fish mouth. This fish's mouth, it is big enough for us to stick inside of it both of our boy heads. This is what we do. We stick our heads into this fish's mouth. When we do do this, when we take us a look up inside of this fish, what we see is, we see our father. It's our father here on the inside of this fish. Our father, he is down inside the belly of this bigger-than-us fish. And us brothers, us seeing our father like this, we both know what it is that we have to do next. I hold up with just one finger to say to our father for him to hold on. What our father does to this is, he holds up his hand too, his thumb and be-quiet finger touching to make themselves into a circle, and in this light that is right now shining down from the above-the-river moon, our father's hand held up in just this making, it makes a shadow of a dog on the inside walls of this here fish. Good, Brothers, is what our father is wanting to say to us, his sons. He winks at us with one of his eyes. With our eyes, us brothers, we look at each other. Brother sticks up and out a thumb. I take this to mean that what Brother is saying is that this big fish, it is a keeper. If you say so, Brother, I say to myself. And then I reach my right hand down inside my right trouser pocket. What I fish out from the inside of this pocket is the knife that us brothers use when we take the fish that we catch out of this dirty river home in buckets rusted with mud. What we do with these fish after we catch these fish, after we walk with these fish back home is: we gut and we cut off the heads off of these fish. We give each of these fish each a name. Not one is named Jimmy or John. Jimmy and John is mine and my brother's name. We call each other Brother. So I take this shining blade of this knife, and then I stick, I run it, the blade of this knife, up from the tail end of this fish all the way up to where this fish's gills are good and red and are about to get even redder now with its own blood. Fish, we say, give us back our father. This, I whisper this. This, to this fish, I hiss this into where I believe is this fish's ear. This big fish, it stiffens, it winces with its fish body, but it's too late now for this fish to put up a fight. The guts of this fish are floating up and away, they are heading down the river, because down and away is how most rivers like to flow. Our river is like most rivers in the way that it flows down and away and out to the lake. But it is up, not down the river, where us brothers want your eyes to take a look: to see, no, not the guts of this big fish floating down and away, down the river, but to look, to see, instead, our father, he is up from this fish's big fish belly, like a last breath bubbling up and out: this is our father coming back upriver back up to be with us. Our father, he is up from the bottom of this muddy river rising up: our father, he is up toward the light of the moon rising up: he is, our father, a fish looking for a hook, and a pole, and a mud-rusty bucket filled up to its brim with fish. He is looking for us brothers for us to take him back home with us. Because he is hungry, our father says to us. He says this to us with his hands. It's time, our father, he knows this—our father, he is telling us brothers this—to come back home to us brothers, to sit back down, a father to us sons: it is time for us to eat.

Our Father is a Fish

We were down by the river, us brothers, fishing for fish, when Boy walked up to tell us what it was that he was dying to tell us: that he'd just seen himself a ghost. This ghost, Boy said it, it wasn't just any ghost, this ghost that Boy said that he'd just seen. This ghost, Boy told us brothers, it was the ghost of a fish. A ghost fish? Brother asked this back, because he wanted to believe it. We wanted to believe that a ghost could be of a fish. That's right, Boy said right back at us brothers. The ghost that I just saw it, this ghost, it was a fish. Where'd you see it, this ghost? was what I wanted to be told. Did Boy see it, this ghost, was what I wondered, down by the dirty river that runs through this dirty river town? Boy saw it, this ghost fish, was what Boy told us. I saw it, Boy said it, out back in the back of your house's backyard. Out back in the back of our house's backyard, there was a telephone pole back there studded with the chopped-off heads of fish. Each fish, each fish's head, us brothers, we gave each one a name. Not one was called Jimmy or John. Jimmy and John was mine and my brother's names. We called each other Brother. Boy, I said to Boy, this boy who was not one of us brothers. Boy, I said this word out loud again. Give me your hand, I said. Take me, I told him. Let me see this thing that you say that you've seen. Boy nodded with his boy head at us brothers and took hold of us by our hands. Us brothers, with Boy in between us, we walked like this back up and back away from the river, we were taken back, by Boy, by our hands, out back into the back of our backyard. Brothers, Boy said to us then, and here he stopped us in our walking up and out back. This is where I saw what I say that I saw, Boy said. Boy let go of us brothers by our hands so he could point up with just one of his hands up to the top of our fish-headed telephone pole, up to where those fish's fish heads gazed down upon us brothers with their eyes and their mouths opened up wide for singing. Up at the top of this fish-headed telephone pole, up to where with his boy hand Boy was pointing up for us brothers to take us a look, we could see a fish's head way up at the pole's top. And this head, up here up at the top, it was the biggest fish head that us brothers had ever fished and it was the biggest fish head we had ever chopped off and it was the biggest fish head that we had ever hammered and nailed with our rusty, bent-back nails into that pole's creosoted wood. Us brothers looked up, but then we looked our looking up look back down and back at each other. There was this look that us brothers sometimes liked to look at each other with. It was the kind of a look that actually hurt the eyes of the brother who was doing the looking. Imagine that look. That fish there, Brother said, and here he took Boy's hand back into his own. That fish, I said, because I knew what Brother was going to say and what Brother was going to do next. That fish head, I then said. That fish, we both whispered into the holes in the sides of this boy's head. This fish is our father, we said. And like this, with Brother holding Boy back up against this back-of-the-yard pole, us brothers, we chopped off this boy's head.

Mud Fish

Those muddy river fish that us brothers used to catch out of the muddy river that runs its way through this muddy river town, those fish were muddy river fish that always tasted of mud. Us brothers, we liked mud and liked the taste that was mud, we liked to eat mud and liked to eat too these muddy river fish. These fish from our muddy river, if it was up to us brothers, we'd let those fish sit overnight in buckets full of the river's muddy water. To us brothers, to our muddy brother eyes, in our mud-eating boy mouths, fish can never be, fish can never taste, muddy enough. If it was us brothers who were the ones in our house doing the cooking up of these muddy river fish, we'd fry those fish up in mud instead of in butter, what our father always liked to call lard. But in our house it was our mother who was the one always doing the cooking. The kitchen inside our house, it belonged to her. But our mother, unlike us brothers and unlike our father too, she never liked the taste of mud, or liked the look of mud. She didn't like it, our mother, when us brothers walked into her mother kitchen with mud caked on the bottoms of our boots. So what our mother would always do to the fish, before she would cook up the fish was, she'd soak them in cold salt water. This, she liked to tell us brothers, would get rid of the fish's muddiness. Mud, our mother liked to say, it was in these fishes' blood. Yes, yes, exactly, was what us brothers wanted to say to our mother. That, we wanted to say, was what made the fish taste, to us brothers, so good. Even if we'd said to our mother what we wanted to say to our mother, our mother, she wouldn't have listened to us. Instead, our mother, she would do to the fish what she always did to our fish. She'd hold our fish under the kitchen's cold tap water the way she used to take hold of us brothers' muddy hands and tell us brothers to scrub, to wash the dirt of the mud off of us. Us brothers, we loved mud. No matter how much our mother made us brothers scrub the mud, the mud, it wouldn't come washing off. It was the same, too, with the fish. No matter what our mother did to try to rid those muddy river fish of their fishy, muddy taste, she could not take the mud of the river out of those fish. Us brothers, our river, it was a muddy river. Our river, us brothers', it was the muddiest river ever made. And those muddy river fish that us brothers used to catch out of this muddy river that runs its way through this muddy river town, those fish were muddy river fish with a muddy river running through the inside of each of these fish. In our river, in our muddy river town, there were so many muddy fishes, there was so much mud in our muddy river, that if you took all of those muddy river fish and if you held all of those fish all together, fish after fish after fish after fish—this, are you picturing this: all of these fish, with the mud of the river running through these fish, these fish, these fish, these fish: they would have made a mud-fish sea. They would have made a sea of fish turn back to a river of mud.

Our Mother is a Fish: Revisited

Our mother is a fish that drowned in the muddy river that runs its rusty nail through our muddy river town. Our river, our town, rusty with mud and smoke and steel, it is more mud than it is river, it is more dirt and mud and smoke and steel than it is town. Us brothers, one day, found our mother washed up on the river's muddy shore, side by side, side-faced, with rusted cans and rusted parts of cast-away metal. Our fish-faced mother was laying face-to-the-side on the right side of her body, her fish body a water-soaked bag of skin and bones with not much else inside it. Our mother's one eye, her left, that was facing up out of the up at us brothers, it was stuck-in-the-mud open and was looking up at us as if it was looking up at us. When I said so to Brother, Brother asked, Looking at us? Why? was what Brother wanted to know. What could she want from us? She wants us, I explained this to Brother, to take her back home with us. Our mother, Brother

104

then set out to explain this to me, is looking at us with what she always looked at us with when she looked her eyes down at us. What I said to this was, What? How? What does she want? What our mother wants from us, Brother, Brother pointed this out, is what she has always wanted from us. I waited to hear whatever it was that Brother was about to say next. She wants us to leave, Brother said. She wants us to go. I'm surprised, Brother said, she's not turning over right now in her muddy grave to see and to know that there's nothing more for her to do. I can fix that, I told Brother. I told this to our mother too, and then I turned our mother over and onto her back. This turning over of our mother, I did this with my foot, my boot, the tip of it, the toe, it was thickly-covered with mud. Look, I said to Brother. Brother listened, then looked. We both did. We looked our fish-of-a-mother right in the other eye. Our mother's other eye, her right one, it was an eye that was missing. The eye's socket, it was a hollowed-out shell stuffed with mud. Us brothers, we gave each other a look. There was this look that us brothers we sometimes liked to look at each other with this look. It was the kind of look that actually hurt the eyes of the brother who was doing the looking. Imagine that look. Here's to mud in your eye, Mother, we said. We raised our hands to salute the moon. And then we did with our fish-of-a-mother what every good fisherman will do to a fish when a fish is found washed up dead on the river's muddy shore. We stuck our dirty boy fingers into our mother, inside our mother's other eye socket, where there was still an eye inside it, and we plucked out our mother's marbly-white eye. Us brothers, we could not the two of us decide which one of us would get to do, with this eye, what we both knew the both of us wanted to do. So we fought. We rolled around in the mud, down by the river, our fish-of-a-mother, our mother's fishy eye, sometimes coming in between us. We fought and we fought and we rolled around in the mud until it was the voice of Girl we heard telling us to stop. We both of us brothers turned because the both of us brothers knew who was doing the telling. It was Girl and not just the voice of Girl telling us brothers to let her settle this between-us brothering. And then it was Girl, it was the hand of Girl, who grabbed our mother's eye away from our fingers. It was then that Girl bit our mother's eye in two. Here, Girl said, to us brothers, and she handed each of us brothers one half of our mother's fish-eyed eye. It was as if Girl was giving to us brothers each one of us half of a moon. Girl said then, Gumball. Then Girl told us to chew. Us brothers, we chewed. We tossed back our mother's bit-in-two eyeball into our boy mouths. We chewed and we chewed but we did not swallow. Our mother's eye, our mother—she was a fish, she was a fish eye, that us brothers did not eat. When we were done doing our chewing, we stuck our mother's chewed-up eyeball onto the bottoms of our muddy boots. Then we clicked our heels three times and walked home from the river, through the mud, into our mother's kitchen. We walked into our mother's kitchen. We did not take off our boots.

The Singing Fish: Revisited

Sometimes, us brothers, we take the fish that we fish out from the dirty river that runs its way through this dirty river town, and we take these fish, into our mud-rusty buckets, back up to the back of our house's backyard, out back to where there is this fish-headed telephone pole back there studded with the chopped off heads of fish. But there are times when, before we gut and before we cut off these fish's fish heads, sometimes we like to take these fish and sometimes we like to line these fish up, in fish rows, out back in the back of our yard. When we line these fish up, in rows of fish like this, out back in the back of our backyard, us brothers, what we do next is this: we take turns stepping, with our boots, gently, onto these fish's beautiful white bellies—to see what kinds of beautiful fish sounds this, these fish, might with their bodies make. Most of the time, when we step, like this, gently, with our boots, onto the bodies of these fish, these fish make come out of their open fish mouths a gasping sound, the sound of a fish's last breath being taken and then taken away. But there are these other times, too, when we step, gently, with us brothers' boots, onto the body of one of these fish, when out of this fish's fish mouth comes a sound that can only be called or said to be singing. When a fish like this begins to sing like this, us brothers, we know there is only one thing for us to do. We drop down, onto our hands and knees, down into the mud, and like this, with our ears pressed down to be close to this fish's singing fish mouth, we open up our own mouths and begin to eat.

Boy's Tongue

One night, us brothers, we are down by the river that rivers its way through this dirty river town, fishing for the river's dirty river fish, when up to us brothers walks that boy who, us brothers, we call this boy Boy—boy born without a tongue on the inside of his boy mouth, that boy Boy, he walks right up to us brothers and in his boy mouth, that hole in his face where Boy used to feed food into, that place where no words, only boy grunts, used to come grunting out of that grunty space, and down there, us brothers, we can see, when Boy opens up that hole of his opened wide open at us brothers, we see a tongue down there in the place where no tongue used to be. What's that? Brother says. Where'd you get that? is what the both of us brothers want to be told. How, we say. When, we ask him. Who'd you get a tongue from? us brothers, with our mouths, we push with our own tongues this mouthful of words out. Like this, the both of us brothers, we poke around with our boy tongues down and around inside our own boy mouths, just to make sure that Boy did not take out *our* tongues from the insides of our mouths. I got it, Boy tells us, I took it, Boy says, and here he is a boy grinning back at us brothers with a big boy kind of a fish-kissing grin. I took it, I got it, I cut it out, Boy tells us, from the mouth, Boy says it, of a fish. A fish, us brothers say this fish word back down at Boy. What kind of a fish? is what we want to be told. Boy holds out his hands out in front of us brothers to show us what kind of a fish this fish was. It was a big fish is what Boy says to us brothers next. It was big, Boy says, and it was silver shining, he tells us, and when I held this fish up in my boy hands the scales from this fish stuck to and glittered back sparkly in my hands. Boy holds his hands up close to us brothers so we can see that his hands, it's true, Boy's hands: they look like they've been dipped in stars. Look with us at Boy. Us brothers, we have this look that we sometimes like to look at each other with. It's the kind of a look that actually hurts the eyes of the brother who is doing the looking. Imagine that look. Come closer, us brothers, we say these words to Boy. Open up, we tell him. Let us take a look inside: to get us brothers a better look at that fish tongue down on the inside of your mouth. Just like this, to us brothers saying for Boy to do so, Boy does what he is told. This boy we call Boy, he takes two steps up closer to us brothers and then he opens up his boy mouth for us brothers to see inside. What we see, when we take this look close into Boy's opened up mouth, we see a tongue down there inside of there that is moving around down there, it is flopping around in there, yes, just like a fish. Open wider now is what us brothers say next to this boy. Then, we say, wider, we say. Open up wide, we say, as wide as you can make your mouth go, we tell him. Here again, Boy does what he is told. Good, Boy, we say to Boy. Boy's mouth, that hole in his face that he used to feed food into, that place where no words used to come mouthing out, it is opened up so wide now, for us brothers to see down inside it, that it is a hole that is swallowing up whole the head that is this boy's whole boy head. Boy's head, it is more of a hole right now than it is a head right now, and Boy, this boy with his mouth opened up wide, he is making sounds come out of this hole in his face, this space with that fish's tongue flopping around down inside it, and this sound, us brothers realize then, it is the sound of a fish that is a fish that it, this fish, it can sing. This fish's fish tongue down inside of Boy's opened up mouth, it is the tongue of a singing fish, and this boy Boy, he is now no longer just a boy, but he is a boy who can sing. Sing, this boy, he is a singing boy, this boy is. And us brothers, hearing these singing sounds coming out from Boy's wide open mouth, we look at each other with that look. There is that look that us brothers sometimes like to look at each other with. It is that look that actually hurts the eyes of the brother who is doing the looking. Look at us brothers looking with this look. This fish here, Brother says, looking at me with this look. It's a keeper, Brother says. If you say so, I say back to what Brother has just said. And just like this, us brothers, with our boy hands fishing down, up to our wrists, down into the insides of Boy's mouth, us brothers, together like this, we pull, we tug, we yank, we rip, this fish, this tongue, this song, out from the insides of Boy's mouth. When Boy sees what us brothers have to him just done, when he sees his fish tongue held out, like a fish, out in the space between us brothers, Boy opens up his mouth to speak, to say to us brothers, What have you just done? and Why would you want to do it?, but nothing, nothing but a grunt, that is, comes out at us brothers grunting out. Boy grunts and he grunts and he keeps on grunting at us brothers, until us brothers, we know there is nothing else for us to do. We reach with our hands down inside our front trouser pockets, to fish out the knives that are down there waiting for us brothers to fish them like this up and out, and then, just like this, with these knives raised up above our own boy heads, we cut, we slice, we chop and we chop, until we chop off this boy's head. Boy's head, down in the mud down here by the river, it is sitting there, down in the mud, the way that only a cut-off head can sit in the mud down by a muddy river's muddy shore. The eyes in Boy's head, they are looking up at us brothers, and Boy's mouth, that hole in his face where Boy used to feed food into, where no mouthy sounds could once upon a time ago come out at us mouthing out, this boy mouth, it is as quiet now as any hole is dark and quiet and making not a sound when it is a hole filled up with mud.

Boy's Tongue: Revisited

And then there was this other time when, us brothers, we fished a fish out from the dirty river that runs its way through this dirty river town, and this fish, when we stuck our knives up inside of this fish, to gut the guts out of this fish, to cut off this fish's fish head, inside of this fish there was a tongue up there inside the insides of this fish. This tongue that was stuck up inside of this fish, it wasn't a fish's tongue up inside of this fish. This tongue, it was too big for it to be a fish's tongue. This tongue, what it looked like to us brothers, it looked like to us brothers that it was a human's tongue, this tongue, it could have been the tongue inside the mouths of one of us brothers. But this tongue, it wasn't the tongue of one of us brothers. Us brothers' tongues, when we opened up our boy mouths toward each other to see inside of each other's mouth, we both of us brothers saw each of us brothers' tongues down on the insides of our mouths. But Boy, that boy born without a tongue in his boy mouth, that boy whose mouth was a hole in his face that he fed food into, that boy who was born with teeth and a full head of hair, maybe this tongue was the tongue that was meant to be born into that boy's mouth. Maybe this fish, maybe it was the fish that was the fish that ate Boy's tongue. Maybe this is why Boy didn't get born with a tongue of his own on the inside of his mouth. Who of us can really say? So what we did, then, was this: we took this tongue that we found on the inside of this fish when we stuck up our knives up inside of this fish, to gut the guts out of this fish, to cut off this fish's fish head, and we went looking to find Boy, to see if maybe this tongue was the tongue that Boy was not born with. When we found Boy, down by the river, Boy was out walking back and forth across the river's muddy water, going back and forth like this, across the river, like a stone skipped between the river's banks. It was as if on each of the river's two sides there were two boys taking turns skipping stones out across the muddy river. When Boy saw us brothers, when we called out to him, Hey, Boy, Boy took off across that river's muddy water like he was part dog, part fish. Boy came running up to us brothers where we were the two of us standing there in the mud along the river's muddy banks with his boy mouth opened up wide and with no tongue inside of it hanging at us brothers out. It's true, us brothers, we were the brothers who taught this boy more than just a few tricks. It was us brothers who taught Boy how to walk on water. It's true, too, that Boy drowned the first time that he walked out. Boy floated face-down, down the river, but then he walked upriver back, back to us brothers. Good, Boy, us brothers said to this boy. We scratched Boy's back. We pulled a bone out from the back of Boy's hand and we threw it out into the river. Boy, we said to Boy. Go fish. Boy took to that muddy river's muddy water like he was part dog, part fish. Boy came walking back to us brothers with that bone sticking out from both sides of his boy mouth and then he flopped his boy body down right in front of us brothers on the river's muddy shore. Yes, just like a fish. Good, Dog, we said to this boy. Boy, we said to this boy, but we did not hold out to him this tongue that we found up inside of this fish. Let us see inside of your mouth, we said. Open up even wider, we said. Boy, being the good boy that he was, Boy did what he was told. Good, Boy, we said to Boy twice more. We scratched Boy's back. We took a bone from the back of Boy's hand and we stuck it inside his mouth, to hold his boy mouth open. Then, what we did next was, we took that tongue that we found stuck up inside of that fish that we fished up from this dirty river that runs its way through this dirty river town, and we stuck this tongue down into the insides of this boy's open mouth. When we did this with this tongue, this tongue, down inside on the inside of Boy's mouth, what happened to Boy was this: Boy, with his mouth opened wide like this, with the bone from the back of his boy hand stuck in his mouth to hold his mouth wide open like this, and with this tongue stuck down on the inside of his wide-opened mouth, Boy, this boy, he started up singing. Boy sang, and he sang, and he kept on with this singing, and then this boy, singing like this, singing like a fish, he would not, he could not, get himself, or get the tongue on the inside of his mouth, to put a stop to his singing. Us brothers, we didn't know what we were going to do, or how we were going to get this boy to stop with this singing, until we turned back away from the river and stood back facing back toward our house. Our house, in our house's backyard, out back in the back of our house's backyard, there was a telephone pole back there studded with the chopped off heads of fish. In the end there were exactly one hundred and fifty fish heads hammered and nailed into this pole's wood. Each one of these fish, each of these fish's fish heads, each one was given a name. Not one was named Jimmy or John. Jimmy and John was mine and my brother's name. We called each other Brother. When us brothers turned back away from the river to face back toward our house, it was then that we knew what we had to do. So we took Boy by his hand, we took this singing boy, back to our backyard, and we walked with this boy up and back until the back of this boy was backed up against this backyard pole. Boy, we said to Boy. It's time to stop all of this singing. And when Boy could not, when this boy did not stop with his singing, even when we took that bone from the back of his hand and pulled it like a tooth from his wide-opened mouth, we knew there was only one thing left for us to do. Brother held Boy's head up against this fish-headed pole. Up above our heads, those fish heads, with their fish mouths open wide, they looked down upon us brothers. Us brothers, we looked down with our heads, we reached down with our hands, down into the fronts of our trouser pockets, to fish out from down inside of there what we knew would get Boy to stop. And like this, with our knives in our hands, us brothers, we chopped off this boy's head.

The Singing Fish: Revisited

There are, in this dirty river town, with this dirty river running through it, fishering men and fishering women who like to fish from boats. But us brothers, unlike all of them, we do our fishing standing on the river's muddy shore. These boats that we see, out on the river, with these fishering people standing up inside them, we see them all day long going up and down the river looking for fish. Sometimes we see these boats and it looks like to us brothers that they are, all of the time, just running up and down the river *looking* for fish and not ever doing any actual fishing. Us brothers, we could never get it into our heads why a fishering man or fishering woman would need a boat for them to fish with. We always figured let the fish come to us. Which is what the fish usually did. But there was a time, one summer, when it seemed like to us brothers that the fish in our river had gone off to be fish in some other river other than ours. Us brothers, we couldn't imagine a river other than ours. We couldn't picture a fish that would want to be a fish in some other river other than *our* river. Our river was a dirty river, it was a good river, us brothers believed, for dirty river fish like ours to be fish in. Us brothers, we loved this dirty river town with this dirty river running through it where we could always run down to it to fish. But there was that summer. That summer, those dirty river fish of ours that we always used to fish from out of this dirty river that runs its way through this dirty river town, it was as if these fish had gone away to be fish in some other dirty river town other than ours. How could they? was what us brothers wanted to know. We didn't want to believe that our fish might be that kind of fish. In the end, about all this, it was wrong for us brothers to think this about these fish. Our fish, they hadn't left our dirty river, our dirty river town. What happened to our fish was this. It was hot, that summer, and the sky, that summer, it never seemed to turn gray with the promise of rain. A river, us brothers, we soon discovered, it needs rain for it to be a river. Just like a fish needs a river for it to be a fish. By midsummer, that summer, when us brothers made our way down to the dirty river where we always ran ourselves down to its muddy banks to fish for our dirty river fish, there was more mud, down there, that summer, than there was river down there. It looked like to us brothers, to our boy eyes, that the river, too, just like our fish, like it too had gone, it was going, away. The river, it was true, it had gotten thinner along its usual muddy banks. And along the banks of this dirty river, there was more dirt, that summer, than there was mud made by the river's water. But the river, us brothers, we believed in this, deep in our muddy brother hearts, it would always be the river to us. No one or no thing could take the river away from us. And the fish, too, us brothers, we believed this: the fish were somewhere out in the river too. Where the fish were, that summer, out in the river, us brothers, we couldn't get ourselves out to. The fish, we found this out, the fish were out in the river's channels, and out farther too out where the river turns east to become the lake. To the river's channels and out into the lake was where our fish had gone off too: not to some other river, but to this other place in the river and out in that other place too—the lake—that the river flowed out to, though both of these places, us brothers, we could not get out to, not without a boat. Us brothers, we didn't have us brothers a boat for us to go out fishing for these fish in, out where the fish were out there in the river's deeper down waters, out where the river's bottom was deeper down, down there in the river where there was more river for the fish to be fish in. We need us a boat, Brother one night, that summer, he pointed this out. Brother was the brother of us brothers who was always saying what the both of us brothers were thinking. Brother was that kind of a brother. We'd been for the past few nights the both of us brothers both of us thinking this thought, though this was the first time one of us said it out loud outside our own boy heads. It was at night when Brother said what he said about us brothers needing us a boat. Up in the sky, that night, the moon was, as it always seemed to be for us brothers, big and shining white. The river, in the moon's light, it was laid out for us brothers like a silver shimmering fish. Us brothers, we needed us a boat. You can say that again was what I said to Brother. And when I said what I said, when I said these words to Brother, that's when it happened. Out there in the river's moonlit night, out there out on the river, there in the river's dark, out of the corners of us brothers' eyes, we saw it: a boat. There was a boat out there out on the river slowly floating down the river. This was a boat floating slowly down the river without any lights on it to light the river's way. Us brothers, we ran ourselves down to the river to see who it was who was out on this boat, to see who it was who was out on the river, at night, in a boat without any lights. But us brothers, even though the moon was big and white, we couldn't see anyone, no fishering man or fishering woman, standing up or sitting down on the inside of this boat. We even called out to it, this boat, Hey, your lights! Both of us brothers hollered out, Turn on your lights! But only the rivery echoes of our own boy voices returned to us from the river's dark. So what us brothers did then was this. We walked out, into the river, across the river's sparkling dark, out to where this dark boat was darkly drifting, out to where this boat without any lights on it was floating down the river on the river's downriver flow. Careful, Brother, Brother said, as the river crept up around our necks, our heads floating, or looking like they were floating, like a couple of chopped off fish heads. Don't drown, Brother said. When Brother said what was in his boy head, I turned then to face Brother in his face. Half of his face was lit up in the moon's lighthouse light. What I said to Brother then was this. Fish don't drown, Brother, I said. To a fish the river is its home. When I said this to Brother, Brother gave me this look. There was this look that us brothers we sometimes liked to look at each other with this look. It was the kind of a look that actually hurt the eyes of the brother who was doing the looking. Imagine that look. Brother's mouth opened up wide like a fish drinking in water. Let's keep on walking then, Brother said to this. And so, us brothers, out into the muddy river, out across the river's water, we walked, and walked, and kept on walking, walking through muddy water, walking out to where this boat, it was floating and floating away. When the river reached up above our boy eyes, above our fish heads, that's when the both of us brothers took in a deep breath. Like this, like fish, us brothers, with the river's muddy water covering us brothers up, us brothers, our mouths opening up, like this we began to sing.

We Did Not Call This Boy Brother

Us brothers, we knew of this other boy who lived in this town, in this dirty river town, though this boy, this other boy, us brothers, we did not call this boy brother. This other boy, he was different from us brothers. He was not one of us. What was different about this boy was, this boy, he'd never been, by the river, born. He died is what we are telling you. This boy died before he had a chance to breathe. This boy, he was a ghost is what we are wanting you to see. This boy, he was a ghost who lived not just down by the river: no, this boy, this ghost of a not-brother, he lived in the river, down at the river's muddy bottom, down where mud goes when it sinks. This other boy, he haunted us brothers—he liked to scare away from us brothers all the river's fish. Sometimes this boy, he liked to make like he was a fish, and he'd take into his boy mouth one of our mud-dipped, minnowy-tipped fishing hooks. This boy, he would tug, and pull, he would hook himself through

121

his bottom lip, and then he would run, this boy would, down along the river's bottom, and this would make us brothers believe that we had, there on the other end of our lines, hooked to our silvery hooks, a real live fish. A keeper, is what we called these fish: a fish big enough for us brothers to eat. But when we'd reel this boy up and in and drag him up ashore to the river's muddy shore, this boy did not make like he was a fish about to be put into a bucket—a fish that was about to be made dead. Fish on! is what this boy, he'd holler up at us brothers, he'd unlip our fishing hooks, he'd spit them down into the mud. Fish off! is what he'd say to us brothers next, before diving head-first back into those muddy waters. But one night, us brothers, we couldn't take it any longer: this boy making like a fish and then this boy getting off and going away from us. This one night, this other boy, he took into his boy mouth our mud-tipped, minnowy-dipped fishing hooks one too many times, so that when we felt that pull, that fishy boy tug, there on the other end of our line, when we reeled him up and in and plopped him down onto the river's muddy shore: on this one night, with this boy looking up all fishy-eyed up at us brothers up from the river's muddy banks, and with this boy already starting to grin at us brothers, Fish on!—what us brothers did different this night was this. We gave each other this look. There was this look that, us brothers, we sometimes liked to look at each other with this look. It was the kind of a look that hurt the eyes of the brother who was doing this looking. Imagine, if you would, that look. What are you looking like that for? is all that this boy could say. Us brothers, we said nothing to this boy asking us this. What we did say to this boy was this. This fish, Brother said, he is a keeper, Brother said. If you say so is what I said to Brother. I nodded my boy head. I wetted with spit and mud my fish-kissing lips. Then I reached inside my rightside trouser pocket and I fished out our fishing knife. This was the knife that us brothers used to gut out the guts of our fish, to cut the heads off of our fish. And this ghost of a boy, this making-like-a-fish boy, he knew what was coming next. He gazed up good and ready when I raised up this knife up toward the sky and held it like that so that, for a moment, the moon was trapped in the glinting of its silvered metal. And with the moon above us watching, the moon above our brother, I called this boy Boy. Boy, I whispered. Boy, I hissed. You are one of us now, I said. Are you ready for this, Boy, I said. Are you sure about this? This boy nodded with his head. If you say so, I said. If you want me to, I said. And then I chopped off his boy head.

The Dress with Girl Not in It: Revisited

We never did get around to telling you about what us brothers did with our mother's dress once it was, by the river, washed up on to the river's muddy shore. What we did with our mother's dress was this: us brothers, we made it lay down flat, down in the river-made mud, down by the muddy edge of the river—we set the dress out, we laid it out smooth, the way our mother would a dress on her bed before she'd decide whether or not to wear it. Not that us brothers knew any thing much to know about dresses. But this dress—our mother's dress—the dress that us brothers, we tugged this dress over the top of Girl's head, that day when we made her, out of the mud, up from the mud—this dress: what we did next with this dress was, we wrung the muddy river out of this dress. We wrung this dress as dry as we could get it, and then we shook this dress out: we smoothed out all of the wrinkles out of this dress, we laid this dress out and down, in the mud, down by the muddy river—this dress with Girl not in it. And after this? After this, what us brothers did was, we stood over, looking down at, staring down into, this dress: to see if we could see Girl anywhere near it. Like this, with us brothers looking down into this dress, we could not see Girl anywhere near inside, or even near the edges, of this dress. And so, us brothers, we got down on our knees. Us brothers, we kneeled with our knees down on top of this dress. But our hands, our hands—we did not know what to do with our hands. So we did with our hands what was the only thing we knew what to do with our hands when we didn't know what else to do with them. Our hands, we stuck them—our hands—into the mud. Now, now that our hands were good and now that they were muddy now, now, us brothers, we knew what to do with our hands now. Our hands, we let our hands go. Go wild is what we told them. Go to where you always wished you could go to. Us brothers, we closed our eyes—to watch them go in their going. The places where our hands did go, the mud on our hands, the muddiness left mud tracks, a trail of muddy stars, up and down the front of Girl's dress. This dress, it was a dress covered up with mud. It was a dress—this dress was—that was made out of mud: it was that muddy. It was so beautiful, this dress, it looked almost good enough now—this dress did—for Girl to be inside it. But wait: I said almost good enough for Girl be inside it. Because the mud that was Girl's skin, this was the muddiest, the most beautiful, dress of all dresses for Girl to be in. This was the dress that us brothers gave to Girl when we made Girl out of mud. This was the dress that us brothers gave to Girl before Brother did what he did after we made Girl: when he left and went back home and went into our mother's closet and when he came back down to the river Brother was holding in his arms an armful of girl clothes. I wanted to take that dress and throw it into the river. I wanted to watch it like a dead fish float away. But now, I didn't know what to do with this dress. Throw it back to the river now? I couldn't do that: not to the river. The river didn't want this dress, then or now. The river spit this dress up onto the river's muddy shore for us brothers to find it. Where Brother got it, this dress—from our mother's closet—I could take it back there. Hang it up there inside to dry. But no, I didn't want to go there, to that inside-our-house place. So what I did was I did this: I got up and I started walking. I walked along side the river. I walked hand in hand with the river. I walked and I did not stop walking until I saw what I was walking toward. There was this tree down there sticking up from, sticking out of, the river's muddy edge. This tree, it looked more like a stick just stuck in the mud than it did a growing up tree. I didn't know what kind of a tree this tree was. I didn't know its name. Though what I knew for sure about this tree was that it didn't look like it was long for this world. It didn't have any leaves on it, this tree. This tree, it was nothing but sticks and twigs. And so this, this is what I did next. I went over to this tree—this tree with no leaves growing from it, this tree that was more stick and twig than it was tree—and with my hands I broke off from this tree some of its branches, some of its twigs, and what I did then was this: I walked back with these twig branches held in my hands over to where our mother's dress was all covered up with mud. I took the twigs that I was holding in my hands and I knelt down with them down near this dress. What I did then was I stuck them, these twigs, one by one, so that they stuck out, as arms stick out, as legs stick out, from those places in a dress, those holes, where arms and legs are meant to stick out. A bird flying high over head, a bird with eyes not so good, that bird might have looked down on this dress, and looking down it might have wondered: what is that girl in the dress doing laying down in the mud? But that same bird, it also might have wondered: I wonder where is her head? So I went out along the river looking for a head to stick out from this dress where a head ought to stick out from a dress. I did not have to walk too far to find what it was I was looking for. I found a fish—it was a dead fish—washed up on the river's shore, its fish eyes still staring wide open like it was still seeing things—even though, in the eyes of this world, this fish, brother, it was dead. But us brothers, we knew what it meant to be better than dead. We knew that when things die they sometimes just then begin to live. And so I picked up this fish into my hand. This fish, brother, let me tell you this: it was alive. In my hands, this fish, it was more than just a fish. I carried it, this fish, over to the dress with Girl not in it: this dress that did not have above it yet, on top of it yet, a head. I placed this fish where the head needed to be. Now this dress, with its fish head and with its twig arms and stick legs: like this, looking down at it, like this: this dress, it looked good enough to eat. And so, us brothers, the both of us brothers, we got down on our hands and knees, on both sides of this dress, and we slipped our boy hands up and under this dress. Here, us brothers, we could feel, underneath here, something here in the mud beating. So we started digging. We dug down into the mud, under this dress, until we found what and where it was. What it was was, it was a drum. It was a drum shaped like a heart. This heart-shaped drum, us brothers, we started to beat it with our fists—we beat it until this dress stood itself up from the mud and this covered-in-mud dress, it started to dance. It danced its way over to where the river was and it danced across the muddy water and it crossed the muddy river over to the muddy river's other muddy side. Not once—unlike our father, unlike us brothers—this dress, it never once looked back.

Our Mother is a Fish: Revisited

One night, us brothers, we heard us a sound, from where we were down standing, down by the banks of the river, fishing with mud for our river's dirty river fish, it was the sound, us brothers knew, of somebody or someone chopping wood. A tree was what us brothers figured it was. But what us brothers thought was a tree, it wasn't a tree. What it was was, getting itself chopped at like this, it was the fish-headed telephone pole out back in the back of our backyard. Into this pole's wood, us brothers, we liked to take the fish that we'd catch out of the dirty river that runs through this dirty river town, and when we'd chop off these fishes' fish heads, us brothers, we liked to take them, these heads, and we'd hammer and nail, these fishes' heads, into this pole's creosoted wood. Us brothers, we liked it, the sound that the hammer made when we'd hammer and pound our rusty, bent-back nails through these fishes' fish heads and into this pole's dark wood. It was a sound that would sometimes make our father step out back into the back of the yard to be with us brothers. Sons, our father liked to call out to us brothers with this word. Us brothers, we'd both turn back our boy heads toward the sound of a father. We'd wait like this to hear what other words might come from out of our father's mouth. It was always a long few seconds. The sky above the river, the sky above the shipwrecked-in-the-river's-mud mill, it was dark and silent. Somewhere, though, us brothers knew, the sun was somewhere shining. You boys remember to clean up before you come back in, was what our father liked to tell us. But it was our mother now who was the somebody who was taking an axe to our fish-headed, back-of-the-yard pole's wood. Us brothers, up from the river, we ran ourselves up to our mother to ask her what did she think she was doing taking an axe to this pole's wood. What does it look like I'm doing? was what our mother said, and she kept on chopping with her axe—with our father's axe—at this pole's wood. Our fish heads, hammered and nailed into this back-of-the-yard pole with rusty, bent-back nails, some of these fishes' heads shook and flinched and then fell from where they had been hammered and nailed by us brothers into this backyard pole's creosoted wood. Us brothers, we looked up with our eyes at these fishes' heads, open-eyed, open-mouthed, and it was like they were singing to us brothers. When we heard what these fishes' heads were singing to us brothers, us brothers, we took our up-at-our-fishes'-heads looks and we looked these looks at each other. There was this look that us brothers sometimes liked to look at each other with. It was the kind of a look that actually hurt the eyes of the brother who was doing the looking. Imagine that look. We looked and we looked and then we opened up our mouths at our mother. Mother, one of us brothers mouthed out loud with our mouth. Fish, the other one of us whispered. These words, we wanted to believe it, would be enough to get our mother to stop her doing. But these words, to our mother, they were just words to our mother. And so our mother, with the axe in her hands, she kept on chopping at this pole's wood. Us brothers, to our mother, we didn't know what we were going to do, or how we were going to get our mother to stop her in her doing, until we looked back up and saw our fish. Our fish, our fishes' fish heads, open-eyed, open-mouthed, they were looking down upon us brothers, they were telling us brothers what it was that we had ourselves to do. When these fish told us brothers what it was that we had to do, us brothers, we knew that this was what it was we had us to do. So us brothers, we took two steps to be with ourselves two steps closer to our mother, and then we reached out to our mother with our hands to take her hands into ours. Mother, us brothers said. Give us your hands, we said. Hold your hands, we said, up against this pole's wood. But our mother, she was not a brother to us brothers. Our mother, she was just a mother. Our mother, because she was just a mother to us, because she wasn't one of us brothers, she wouldn't do with us what we'd just told. Bad, Mother, us brothers hissed into her mother ears. Us brothers, we looked with our eyes at our mother. We looked with our eyes at our mother the way that we sometimes liked to look with this look at the fish that we liked to fish out of the dirty river that runs through this dirty river town. This fish here, Brother said, and he looked back at me with that look. She's a keeper, was what Brother said. If you say so, I said back to Brother. And then I took that axe out from our mother's hand, this axe that was our father's, and then I chopped off our mother's head.

The Moon is Girl's Heart

We see Girl. We see Girl standing knee deep in the river washing her girl hair in the river's muddy water. Girl, we holler up. Hey Girl, we say, and we run ourselves up to get us brothers a closer look. Girl turns back around toward the sound of our boy voices, but she does not stop her in-the-river washing. Rivers river down from Girl's rivery hair, rivering down the rivery banks of her rivery girl body. Boys, she says to us brothers, and she drops down on her girl knees. Come close, Girl says to this. Listen. When Girl tells us brothers to come close, come listen, us brothers, we always listen. Hear it, Girl says again, and she lifts us brothers up, and holds us brothers up against her heart. We listen, and we listen some more, but there is no sound, there is no beating there, for us brothers to hear. So we lean our ears back away from that soundless place on Girl's body where Girl's heart is supposed to be beating. It used to be there—that beating sound—beating beneath that place on Girl's body, there where there is a freckle right there shaped like a star. Dig here is what our ears used to always hear the heartbeat of Girl whispering to us. But now, us brothers, we don't say a thing to Girl about the quiet we now hear. What we do is we do this: we reach inside with our dirty boy hands, into Girl's made-out-of-mud body, and we take hold of Girl's heart. Girl's heart, we know, because we made it so, it is made out of mud. But the mud, we see now, it has turned to dirt. Girl's heart, it is so hard it is hard for us brothers to touch it. But still, us brothers, we touch it. We touch it, and then we do more than touch it. We take it, Girl's heart, into our dirty boy hands. And what we do then is we pull, and we pull. We give Girl's heart our best boy tug. Yes, Girl's heart, when we tug it like this, it pops loose like a tooth with no roots to it. Girl doesn't wince, or flinch with her girl body, or make with her girl mouth the sound of a sister crying out. Good, Sister, we say to Girl. What we do then is we take Girl's heart and we lower it down into the river. We hold it down underneath the river until the dirt of it turns back to mud. When Girl's heart is back to being mud, we take it, Girl's heart, and we shape it, with our hands, so that it is shaped into the shape of a heart. But no, that's not right, Brother points this out. Girl's heart, it was never shaped the shape of a heart. Brother is right. Good, Brother, I say. And so, like this, us brothers, we make it right. We take our boy hands, we take Girl's heart into our muddy brother hands, and we make it into the moon. The moon, it is Girl's heart, I say. I say this to the sky. Then Girl tells us brothers take a look inside. We do. We look inside. Inside of Girl's moon heart, inside her made-out-of-mud heart, there are two sisters. One for each of us brothers. Us brothers, we look and we look and then we dive inside. When we do, this moon, it shatters into a billion pieces. Each broken piece becomes a star.

Boy's Tongue: Revisited

One day Boy, that boy born without a tongue on the inside of his boy mouth, he walked up to us brothers, down by the river where us brothers we were standing doing us our fishing, and he held out to us brothers his boy hand closed up like it was to make itself into a fist. For you, Brothers, Boy mouthed these three words out, and then he opened up his closed-up fist. In Boy's hand, Boy held out to us brothers what looked like to us to be Boy's tongue. He held it, like this, in his hand, like you would a fish out of water, Boy held it out, like this, out for us to see it like this, the way you might hold a fish too small to keep. That's what Boy's tongue, sitting there in the palm of his boy hand, that's what it, Boy's tongue, looked like to us brothers: like a fish too small to keep. But what would us brothers do when a fish too small to keep had died in our boy hands, had breathed its last breath with one of our silvery fishing hooks hooked deep down into the insides of its fish belly? Sometimes what us brothers would do to a not big enough fish like this, we'd walk with it, in our hands, out into the river, and we'd hold it, like this, in the river, like this, until the river's muddy waters brought the fish back into its own life. It was the river that taught us brothers this: that nothing ever really dies. So, us brothers, we walked, like this, with Boy's tongue, in our hands, out into the river's muddy waters. We held it, this fish, us brothers, like this, into the river, under the river's muddy water, and we stood there like this, we watched Boy's tongue, like this, it just laid there, like this, songless, in our hands, our hands with the river flowing between them, until all of the fish that live and swim in the river, they swam up to it, this dead fish of a tongue, and what they did then, these fish of the river, these fish that were still very much alive, they opened up with their fish mouths and, no, they did not start to sing, though it's true that us brothers, this is what we wanted them to start to do: no, what they did, then, these fish, was, these fish, they opened up their mouths and started to eat. These fish nibbled with their fish mouths on the tip of Boy's dead fish of a tongue as if it was a fish left there for them, given to them like this, by the river for them to eat it—this, to keep this dead fish in some way alive. There were fish lined up upriver from where, us brothers, we were standing, out there in the middle of the river, all the way up to where the steel mill, it was sitting all quietly shipwrecked in the riverbank's rivermade mud. By the time the moon rose, it was just barely rising up out of the river, there was nothing more left of Boy's tongue for us brothers to hold onto. Us brothers, when Boy's tongue, when there was nothing left of it for us to hold onto it with, we walked back out of the river and we headed ourselves back to the back of our backyard. We were on our way back to the back of our backyard, with our buckets half empty of fish, when we heard a sound, it was calling us brothers, Go back, brothers, go back and to the river go. When we turned back toward that sound and walked ourselves back to where the river was, we could see that this sound, it was the fish in the river making these go to the river sounds. Boy walked up to us then, again, and he stopped and he stood in front of us brothers, his face facing away from the river, and then, like this, Boy opened up his mouth at us brothers to speak. Boy's mouth, that hole in his face that he fed food into, that hole where sometimes some mouthy sounds might come grunting out, in that hole, when Boy opened it up at us brothers, like this, inside of it, us brothers, we could see what we knew it, it was a fish, there on the inside of Boy's mouth, right in there where a tongue, a tongue there ought to be. When Boy opened up his mouth like this at us brothers, Boy and the fish on the inside of his boy mouth, they started to sing, the both of them, like this, Boy and Boy's fish tongue, they were singing into the faces of us brothers. Us brothers, standing there like this, we gave each other a look. There was this look that us brothers, we sometimes liked to look at each other with this look. This look, it was the kind of a look that actually hurt the eyes of the brother who was doing the looking. Imagine that look. This boy here, Brother said, looking at me with this look. This fish here, Brother said to me. They're a couple of keepers, Brother said. If you say so, I said to Brother. And then I fished out my fishing knife from inside my trouser pocket, and I cut off this boy's head.

Man

We are down by the river, just the two of us brothers, standing down by the river's muddy edge, us brothers every once in a while reaching down with our boy hands to pick up some rock up from the riverbank's mud, to skip these rocks out into the river's muddy water, when out of somewhere comes this man—Man, us brothers, we will come to call this man—this man comes walking up from behind us brothers, and this man Man, in his man hands, he has two fishing poles sticking out from his big man hands. Man stops in his walking up to us brothers and he stops and stands in front of us brothers, and then Man turns his man back to the river to face off his face with the both of us boys. For you, Boys, Man says, and he holds out from in his man hands these two fishing poles toward us brothers. Go on, take them, this man tells us. They're yours. But why? and then, What for? are the questions that us brothers ask of this man. To fish with is what this man says to this. We know this, we say, but why would you think to give two fishing poles to us? Man, this man, he gives us two brothers this look at us brothers like he is the man who made us brothers us. Sons, Man says to us. Let me tell you a thing or two about rivers, this man says. A river, Man tells us, when you're down by a river, Man says, you've got to be doing more than just standing there, down by the river, watching the river go on by. Us brothers, us who know this, we give this man a look. You think you can show up one day and tell us brothers what a river is for? is what we are looking at this man with this look. We'll tell you a thing or two, we want to tell this man, we'll show you a thing or two, we wish to say, about what a river is to be used for: we think all of this but we do not say it. Fish is what this man says to us brothers next. To fish with, and this man, he unhooks the silvery hooks hooked to the eyes of these two sticking out from his hands fishing poles and these hooks dangle and hang there looking back at us as if us brothers are a couple of fish. The poles' silver hooks shine out at us brothers with the shimmery light of something never before seen. Let's just say, this man says, that I handed you boys a fish, and with this Man digs down with his big man's hand into his jacket pocket and he fishes out from inside of it a fish. This fish, with its fish eyes looking out at us brothers, it gives us brothers a look. This fish's open mouth, it is with its fish mouth telling us brothers what to do with this man Man. You boys, this man goes on moving with his mouth, you boys could take this fish from out of my hand and take it home right now to fry it up and eat it. Us brothers, us nodding our boy heads yes, we know that this much is true, what this man Man is saying to us, but we look up at this man, with our eyes widening into moons, as if this is all something brand new to us. But what about tomorrow? is what this man says to us brothers next. And what about the day after tomorrow? Man stands there, like this, with this fish held up in his one hand, waiting for us brothers to say what about the day after tomorrow. Us brothers, we don't say anything to this man to what about the day after tomorrow. Us brothers, we don't like to think too much about tomorrow. Us brothers, we are brothers who live in the today. Us brothers, we are brothers who like to wait for tomorrow to come before we start to think at all about it. Man looks his man look down at us brothers and then he gets his mouth ready again to speak. But if I were to give you boys each one of you boys a fishing pole and not just a fish, if I were to teach you boys how to fish, you boys can fish for and you boys can catch fish and eat fish everyday for the rest of your boy lives. Us brothers, the both of us brothers, we nod yes with our boy heads to the picture, to the possibility, of this: we are licking our lips to the thought of this. That sure is a long time is what Brother then says to this. When Brothers says this, this man, Man, with these two fishing poles in his hands, with that fish that he fished out from the inside of his jacket pocket gripped by its gills in one of his hands, this man, he shakes his man head to Brother saying this. Man looks his man eyes down at Brother and he says to us brothers, That's what you think is what this man says. Before you boys know it, this man says, you two boys will be old just like me. Us brothers, we cannot picture this and so we know that this, it is not true. There will be boys, Man says, who will walk up to you and call you Mister. Man says, There will be little girls who will tug on your sleeve and say, Sir, would you like to buy a box of cookies? To this, to even just the thought of this, we set this man straight. Man, this man who we call Man, he doesn't know what he's saying. This man Man, this man doesn't know who he's talking to when he's talking like this to us brothers. Man, this man, he doesn't realize that the two boys who he is right now talking to are the two of us brothers. This man thinks that we are just boys who will one of these days, like Man said that we would, grow up to be grown-up men. This man, Man, he doesn't know the first thing about what it means to be a brother. And so, us brothers, we go ahead and we tell him this. That's what you think is what we go ahead and we tell this to this here man. You don't know who you are right now talking to, we say. Us brothers, we give each other this look. There is this look that us brothers, we like to look at each other with this look. It is the kind of a look that actually hurts the eyes of the brother who is doing the looking. Imagine that look. Brother looks this look away from us looking this look and then he says, to the river, to the fish, to the mud that holds this dirty river in its dirty river place: Brother says, to all of this: This man here, Brother says. He's a keeper, Brother says. If you say so, I say to this. And then just like this, us brothers, we fish with our boy hands down into our front trouser pockets, we fish out from deep inside of this place the knives that we know are down there waiting. And then, together like this, us brothers, we raise our boy hands up to be closer to sky, we cut the moon that is always so full into two half-moon pieces, we look this man Man right in his man's eye, and then we chop off his man head.

Girl

Us brothers, we love the sound of that word girl so much that one day, out of nowhere, we start calling everything we see, Girl. Let's go, Girl, we say, to each other. Let's go down to the girl, one of us brothers will go to the other, and to the river is where we go. Let's catch us some girl, the other brother will then say to this, and we'll grab us our fishing poles and a muddy bucket of worms and into the river us brothers fish. Girl sure is girly, one of us will point this out, pointing with a finger at the muddy river flowing past our feet. After a while, after we fill our buckets up with a whole mess of girl, one of us brothers will say, Sister, I'm hungry. Let's go fry us up some girl. Like this, us brothers, we go back and forth between us, girl this and girl that, until it is raining girls and girl. The moon in the sky is girl. The sky and the mud is girl. It's us girls walking round this girl town with girl dripping from our lips, girl this and girl that, until bottles and buckets and rusty trucks and trains, until hammers and fish heads and bent-back nails—all of these things come rushing up to us brothers, all of them drawn to us by the sound that those four letters make: G-I-R-L. But girl the way that girl was meant to be spelled: with twelve r's, thirteen u's, and twenty-thousand l's at the end of girl, stretching across the earth.

What We Tell Girl to Do with Us Brothers If We Ever Stop Making Mud

Bury us brothers here. Cover us up with the mud of this river. Let this muddy river run up and over us brothers, let it run its muddy waters up into the insides of our mouths. Let the fish of the river, let the mud too, nibble and gnaw us brothers down to bone. And the weeds of this river, those flowers growing up from the river's rivery bed, let them wrestle and wrap us brothers up into their leafy arms: so that we might be held here, down at the river's muddy edge, down here where there are stones for us to turn over, with our fingers and toes, stones for us to up from the mud pick up for us to throw: so they can float back up to that rivery hand, so they can rise up into that rivery sky—that nest of stars they fell out from back when they, the fishes of this river, back before they turned into birds, first learned how to fly.

The Man Whose Guitar was a Fish

There was this man in our town, this dirty river town, who used to come into town to play his guitar, on street corners, outside of bars, down by the river even, him and his guitar standing and sparkling in the spotlight of the moon, and he'd play that guitar of his as if it was some fish fished out of some river unknown to us brothers, some other river other than the dirty river that runs its way through this dirty river town. This man who played this guitar of his like it was some kind of a fish, he was not our father, though there were times, like when he was closing his eyes and singing, when we wished that maybe he was, our father. What this man was, this man who sang and played his guitar like it was some kind of a fish fished out of some river unknown to us, this man, he was not our father, but what he was was, he was our father's brother. Our father, our father who did not sing or play the guitar, our father who liked to fish, our father who walked down to the river, one night, he walked out into the river, he walked out across the river, one night, and did not come walking back: our father did not call this brother of his Brother the way that us brothers do. Our father, what our father called his brother was, he called his brother Joe. Hey, Joe, we'd hear our father say. But this Joe, our father's brother who our father did not call him Brother the way us brothers call each other Brother, this Joe never said anything, he never gave any words to our father back. Sometimes this Joe, our father's brother, he would break out into song when he heard his brother's voice, our father's, calling out to him, Hey, Joe. But most of the time, our father's brother, he was quiet. Sometimes, he would just be standing there and we wouldn't even know it. Sometimes, it made us brothers think that maybe this Joe, our father's brother, was, like Boy, born without a tongue on the inside of his mouth. Maybe when he sang, maybe to be able to sing like our father's brother was able to sing, maybe the sounds that he made with his mouth came from some other place deep inside his man body. Maybe those sounds had nothing to do with being born with or born without a tongue inside his mouth. Or maybe our father's brother didn't give any words back to our father, maybe he acted like he didn't hear it when our father said to him, Hey, Joe, maybe he was sometimes deaf, or maybe our father's brother sometimes didn't say any words back to our father calling to him, Hey, Joe, because Joe, Joe was not our father's brother's name. What our father's brother's real name was, it was Hank. But our father was the first to say, to this brother of his, that there were already too many guitar-singing singers in this world who go by the name of Hank. So Joe was the name that our father called his brother by. Hey, Joe, our father would say. And so Joe was what us brothers, Joe was what our father and our mother and the rest of the townspeople who lived in our town, Joe was what we all called our father's brother by whenever we called him, which wasn't very often, because Joe liked it best to be left alone with just himself and his guitar that he played as if this guitar was some sort of a fish. But to us brothers, after a while, to our brother ears, the name Joe didn't sound right, not for our father's brother, not for this man who could make his guitar and make with his mouth, or make come out of his mouth, a sound that sounded, a sound that sang out, just like a fish. So us brothers, what we did was, when we wanted to call out to our father's brother was, we called him Uncle Fish, because him being a brother to our father made him be an uncle, our mother explained it, to us. But sometimes, too, us brothers, we liked to call him Uncle Guitar with our boy mouths making a loud hard g-sound when we said that word guitar, like gee-tar, or sometimes, when we had the breath inside us to make our mouths say it, we'd call him, our father's brother, our uncle, The Man Whose Guitar was a Fish. It wasn't *really* a fish, this guitar, but it sometimes, to us brothers, looked like it was, the way its sparkly guitar body and silvery steel strings used to shimmer and shine and shoot back out at us moonlight when our father's brother, when Joe, when Hank, when Uncle Fish, when Uncle Guitar, when The Man Whose Guitar was a Fish, used to strum with his big-knuckled hand across its mouth to make that guitar and its six steel strings sing and sing and sing. But one night, when us brothers saw The Man Whose Guitar was a Fish standing outside our town's hardware store with old Mister Higgerson there on the inside of there standing on his one leg that he still had left with him from back when he was getting shot at in the war, we saw that Uncle Fish, Uncle Guitar, The Man Whose Guitar was a Fish, he was on this one night just standing there doing nothing there but just standing there outside of old Mister Higgerston's hardware store's window: he wasn't singing with his mouth, his guitar, it wasn't humming with its six silvery strings, because our father's brother, The Man Whose Guitar was a Fish, he didn't have his guitar strapped or wrapped around the hunchback of his back. Hey, Uncle, us brothers called out to him when we saw him, our father's brother, our Uncle Hank, this uncle of ours who wasn't much of an uncle to us: he wasn't, we didn't think, much of a brother to the man who was our father—this man who, our mother sometimes said, to our father, our mother sometimes said that this uncle of ours was crazy—what our mother called this uncle was she called him Crazy Hank, because our mother, she sometimes said that our father's brother had too much moon shine running through his veins. Us brothers, the first time we heard our mother say this about our father's brother, our uncle Hank, we figured that this, that having the shine of the moon running through his veins, this had to be a good thing, that maybe this was what made our father's brother's guitar sound the way that it did when he strummed it with his hand and made its strings start up singing. But our father told us brothers that when our mother said that his brother had too much of the moon's shine running through his veins, she wasn't talking about the moon at night and its shining, which he knew us brothers loved the moon almost as much as we loved the river and the mud that held the muddy river in its place, not to mention the fish in this river that us brothers loved so much to catch. What our father told us, what our mother was *really* saying about our uncle, The Man Whose Guitar was a Fish, was that he was most of the time always drunk, that the whiskey he liked to drink, he liked to make it himself, down in the basement of the house where he lived with no one but himself. When we saw our uncle Fish, Uncle Guitar, The Man Whose Guitar was a Fish, standing out there out on the street's corner without his guitar, we knew that something was up, that something had gone wrong. Hey, Joe, us brothers, we called out to our father's brother. Hey, Uncle, we said. We did not say Uncle Hank. What we said was, Your guitar, we said. It's gone, we said. Where'd it go? we then asked as if this guitar was a fish that could get up and get away, as if it was a dog that could walk out one night on a night with no moon or stars shining down and go to sleep in a place, across the rusted rails of a railroad track say, that was never meant for sleeping dogs to go to sleep there.

Our father's brother looked at us brothers with a look on his face that made us believe that, at first, he didn't know that it was us. It's us, we told him. It's Jimmy, I said. And John, Brother said. And when we said this, these names, us brothers, we gave each of us brothers a look. There was this look that us brothers, we sometimes liked to look at each other with this look. It was a look that actually hurt the eyes of the brother who was doing the looking. Imagine that look. Now imagine the looks on us brothers' faces when Uncle Guitar, Uncle Fish, The Man Whose Guitar was a Fish, looked at us brothers and he told us brothers that it, his guitar, he gave his guitar away. It was time, he told us, to let it go. So I threw it back, was what our father's brother told us. *Gave it to who? Let it go where? Threw it back how?* This was what us brothers wanted to be told. Us brothers, we were this Joe's closest thing he had to kin, to somebody who you'd give a thing like a guitar to if you were looking for someone to give away a guitar to. And so, us brothers, when we heard him say, To the river, us brothers, we both of us turned to face at each other—we did not have to say a word between us brothers of what we had to do next—and then the both of us brothers turned and we ran ourselves down to the river without saying to this uncle of ours a word or a sound that might sound like a goodbye. When we got down to the river, there was this sound there that, us brothers, we heard, and this sound that we heard, it was a sound that sounded better to our ears than the sound that could be called singing. Us brothers, we looked and we looked but we could not see where this sound was coming from—this sound that sounded better to us than a sound that could be called singing, this sound that was better than fish singing, us brothers, we figured that maybe this sound that the river was making wouldn't mind another kind of a sound to be with it. So us brothers, we dropped down, into the mud, down at the river's muddy edge, and out of this mud, us brothers, we made us a drum. This drum, made out of mud, us brothers, we made it the shape of the moon. We started beating it, with our boy hands, and making, with our hands, a sound come out from this drum that was made out of mud that made the sound that we heard sound out louder, so that this sound it seemed like to us that it was up closer now to us brothers, and when the moon came out of hiding from behind a sky that was muddy with night now, we could see, out on the river, our father's brother's guitar, it was shining in the moonlight there, it was floating down the river out there, it was, out there out on the river, it looked like to us like a raft made out of a steel that it would never, it could never, turn to rust. We watched it float down the river, and then, us brothers, we ran down the river after it, and as we ran, us brothers, we were the both of us brothers with our boy mouths singing. It was us brothers singing that made this guitar stand up on its neck and stop its floating down the river away. When it heard the sound of us brothers singing, this guitar, it started to float back, against the river's current, it was swimming, this guitar was, like a fish, it was coming back to us. This guitar, like a fish, it swam right up to where us brothers were standing, right there on the river's muddy bank, and then it flopped itself down into the mud right there at our feet. This guitar, this fish, us brothers, we picked it up like a fish and lifted it up out of the mud like a fish and we carried it like a fish up and away from the river. This fish, it was too big of a fish to fit inside any of our fish buckets. But we took it with us, this fish, back into town with us, this fish, to where our father's brother, our uncle, Uncle Fish, Uncle Guitar, The Man Whose Guitar was a Fish, back to where we had left him standing, out front in the front of old Mister Higgerson's hardware store window, and when he saw that it was us, when he saw us holding in our hands between us what it was we were holding up and holding out for him to take, what our father's brother said to us was, What's this? Us brothers, we shook our heads at this man who was our uncle. Not what, Uncle, we said. It's who, we said. This, we said, and we held our hands up higher and closer in to our uncle, this here is your son. This here is our cousin. But us brothers, us brothers said, we're gonna call him Brother. Brother because he is one of us. Our father's brother, Joe, Hank, this man that our father did not call Brother, he shook his head at us no. Boys, he said, I know you two are brothers, he said, and yes, when he said this to us brothers, us brothers, we could both of us in the moon's light see, that this uncle of ours did have on the inside of his mouth a tongue just like the both of us. I am not, our father's brother said this much to us, a father. I am, he told us what it was that he was, just a man. And just like this, this man, our father's brother, our uncle, call him Hank or Joe, Uncle Guitar or Uncle Fish, this man, is what we are trying to tell you, this man whose guitar, it was a fish—he fished his hand down inside his trouser pocket. When he pulled it back out, his hand, it was, this hand, a star-shaped knife. And even though us brothers tried to stop him from this doing, even though we sang out for him to stop, he raised back his hand, he brought this hand back forward, he cut off this fish's head.

The Moon is a Fish Eye

Let us brothers tell you this: that if you have never lived to look a fish up close into its eye, then you have never before lived. A fish's eye, when you look up into it, eye to eye, you will see that this eye, it really isn't an eye at all. What it is, a fish's eye is, it is a moon. The first time that us brothers came to see this, we were just a couple of boys getting ready to chop the head off of a fish. I held onto that fish. I held that fish's head down. Brother was the brother of us brothers who took his fish-cutting knife and with this knife that we used to chop off the heads off of our fish and to gut the guts out of our fish, Brother took his knife and he stuck it, this knife, into this fish's eye. When Brother did this with his knife, when he stuck the tip of his knife into this fish's eye, this fish eye—are you picturing this with us?—this fish's eye, in front of our own eyes, it shattered into a billion pieces. Each broken piece became a star.

Boy, Falling

One night we see Boy. Boy, he is down by the river, and what Boy is doing there, down by the river there, is Boy is climbing up the side of Girl's leg. Boy, he is going up: this, us brothers, we can see this. Boy is heading up to the top to where Girl's head, it is sticking up through the clouds, through to that muddy blackness there on the other side of sky. When us brothers see this, back from where we are watching this, back from in the back of our house's backyard, we run ourselves down to the river, so that Boy can hear us when we yell up to him, Hey, Boy, we holler this out. Boy, what do you think you're doing? When Boy hears that it is us brothers who are calling this out, Boy turns back his boy head toward the sound of our boy voices. Yes, Boy, he looks down to see that it is us brothers, but no, Boy does not stop climbing up even when he sees and knows that it is us, even when he hears that it is us brothers who are calling out and up to him to stop.

So us brothers, what us brothers do is, we start too climbing up the side of Girl's leg. Boy, we are going up after Boy to get Boy to come down. It does not take us brothers long for us to catch up to where Boy is just a freckled spot, to where Boy is just a climbing speck of a spider climbing up the side of Girl's mud body. Yes, us brothers, we are boys bigger than this boy Boy is. We are bigger and we are stronger and we are faster climbers-up than this boy. We are boys who know Girl's body, the bumps and rivery curves, better than we know the banks of the river. Us brothers, we know this mountain of mud better than Boy could ever get to know it, because us brothers, we are the brothers whose muddy boy hands made Girl rise up out of the mud. And so, when we get up to where Boy is about half the way up to Girl's mud-topped top, us brothers, we put a hand on each of Boy's shoulders, and this is what gets Boy to stop. Where are you going? is what we say to Boy. And then, Who told you you could? What Boy says in answer to this is, Boy says, Girl. Girl, Boy tells us, told me to come see. Us brothers, our ears, we cannot believe it that this is what Boy is saying, though believe it, we have to believe it: us brothers, we know that it's true that nothing along this river is impossible. We have to believe it too when Girl tilts down her chin at us brothers and nods with her girl head that yes this is true, Girl was the one who told Boy that he could come up to take a look, to see this other piece of the sky. Girl's eyes, when she looks down at us brothers, Girl's eyes are quarter moons that do not wish to be, by us brothers, fully seen. But what Girl wishes to be true, when it comes to us brothers, us brothers, we always do whatever we can to make what Girl wishes for to be true. And so, us brothers, we turn and look the other way. If this is what Girl is wishing for for us brothers, we say this to each other, we say this with this look of us looking the other way. If this is what Girl wants, we look with this look at each other. And like this, us brothers, we nod with our heads okay. And then, like this too, we lift up our boy hands up off of Boy's shoulders and we send Boy back up on his way back up to the top of Girl. Boy, our hands they are saying, Boy, and we both of us brothers both let with our hands go. Go, Boy, is what our hands say. You can keep climbing up. But our legs: our legs are telling another story. Our legs, on us brothers, our legs, they are telling us brothers to climb up too. Go after Boy is what our legs are telling us to do. To our legs, us brothers, we listen up. We go climbing up the side of Girl's leg up after Boy. We do not stop this climbing up, all three of us together climbing up the side of Girl, until we get up to the top that is the top of Girl's head. Up here, Boy reaches down and gives us brothers each a hand up. Up here, us boys, the three of us boys together, us brothers with Boy in between us like this, we make a crown of boys with our boy bodies up here at the top of Girl's head. Boy, he is looking like he is believing that he is one of us. This boy Boy, he could be one of us brothers, or so it might look, but no, this boy Boy, he is a boy who is brother-less. But maybe, us brothers, we are both of us brothers thinking. Us brothers, we are looking at each other, and we are each of us thinking what the other one of us is not afraid to say. What we say to Boy, then, is we say jump. Jump? Boy asks, with his eyes. Jump, we say, with our mouths, but Boy just gives us both this look like Boy believes that us brothers, we are just saying this word just to say it. But us brothers, we keep on looking at Boy with this look and then, us brothers, what we say next to Boy is fly. Fly, we say. Like a bird, we tell him. Boy gives us brothers this look that he is looking at us with. It's a look that is broken only by Boy's eyes blinking both of them at the same time shut. Each blink of Boy's eyes is saying to us brothers, What do you mean? Close your eyes is what we say to this. And this time Boy listens. Boy does what us brothers say. Good, Boy, we say to this. Now, look now: Boy is right now more than just a boy to us brothers. Boy is about to become a brother to us. Now take a deep breath, we say, and we see Boy's body rise up: it is a kite that has just caught hold of a wind that only it can see. Now, we say next, let go, we tell him, and we give Boy with a hand on his back a push. It's a soft push that is just hard enough to get him to walk forward, a step into the dark, and when he opens his eyes what it looks like to him is, it looks like to him like the sky is a sky that is falling up. But what is really going on is this: it is Boy who is the one doing the falling, and this boy, he is falling and falling down fast. Boy is falling fast, down to where the river and the mud that the river makes are waiting to catch his falling. See Boy falling this fall. His falling, it is a sight that is beautiful to see: the way the sky around Boy, that blackness that seems to hold the moon and stars in their place, it unfolds its hands and lets Boy go. Watch Boy go. Boy, he is going. Go, Boy, go, the both of us brothers sing this out. When Boy hits the river, there is this sound that the river makes, it's this sound that sounds like what mud sounds like when you take up a fistful of mud and throw it, this fistful of mud, up against the side of something hard: a wall, a boat's hull, a tree. But there is this moment, too, just before Boy falls, that moment when Boy and Boy's boy feet are about to step off the ledge of Girl's head, when Boy is standing up in mid-air. Boy, it looks like to us brothers that this boy, he is a boy floating in a river of mud. His boy hands are stretched out at his boy side and Boy, this boy—are you seeing with us brothers?—he is pulling in at the sky, he is holding the sky in close to his body, he is pressing it, the sky, and the moon and stars in it, up against his heart. When he does, the moon, it shatters into a billion moon pieces. Each broken piece becomes a star.

We Make Mud: Revisited

We run around town, with mud in our buckets, and cover our whole town up with mud. When the town men and town women come up to us brothers to ask us what do we think we are doing, what us brothers do is, we cover up with mud their wide open mouths shut up. The mud in their mouths, this shuts them up good, this keeps them from asking us brothers what is, to us, a question too stupid of them to be asking. What we are doing—isn't it out in the open, what we are doing? You don't even need eyes in the back of your head to see what it is we are doing. What we are doing is, we are making our town, this dirty river town, we are turning this town back to what it was—back in the beginning, back when all things were made out of mud. Us brothers, we get our mud, we make our mud, down by the muddy river, down where water and dirt meet to make mud. The muddy river is where we come running down to it to fill up our buckets when our buckets are in need of more mud. What we do then is, we run back up through town and run our muddy hands over whatever our eyes can see: houses and churches, bars and donut shops, liquor stores and hardware stores and the building where, inside, the sheriff, it seems to us, he is always sleeping. Inside these town places, the towns people of this town, they stare out at us brothers with a look that says, look what those boys are doing. Us brothers, we look back with a look that says, look again: this is what we are doing. And with our hands dripping with mud and with more mud, we cover them up with mud. We do not stop this covering up, us brothers, we cannot stop mudding it up, not until all of this dirty river town is good and muddy with mud covered up. We build humpbacked hills of mud where once there stood rows upon rows of single-storied houses. And if you look over there, up the river a bit, upriver from where the black husk of the steel mill sits shipwrecked in the mud, this is where, us brothers, we make us a mountain made out of mud. The mill too, us brothers, we cover it up with mud, so that only the rusted tops of the smokestacks can be seen up from the mud sticking up. These smokestacked tops, they are our town's clocktower steeples where, us brothers, we climb up with our muddy buckets dangling empty from our fists, our hands hanging hammerless, our faces gazing up at a mud-colored moon that is half made out of light, that is half made out of mud, until us brothers reach up with our hands, we push up on our toes, and turn out the light.

Mud Love

We each of us brothers each take into each one of our hands a hammer and a handful of rusty, bent-back nails, and we run around town one night nailing and hammering all of the unnailed things that we see around town: boots and buckets, baseball gloves and fishing rods, bikes and kites and rowboats that no longer float, sandboxes, fish nets, little girl dolls without any clothes on, garden hoses, swimming pools, lawnchairs and barstools, baseballs, basketballs, horseshoes and stacks of magazines, books, typewriters, boxes filled with birth certificates, baby pictures, postcards and poems, love notes scrap-paper-scribbled by the hands of faceless names, baby strollers, rollerskates, knapsacks and sleds, dusting brooms, spare tires, chairs that rock in the wind: one by one we each of us each take these things into the hands of us brothers, and we nail these things, and other things too—dog houses, barbecues, sleeping bags and tents (have we yet mentioned fish? fish heads? fish eyes that never stop staring?), milk crates, wooden ladders, mud-crusted shovels, frayed pieces of rope. Get the picture? And last but not least, us brothers, we take hammer and we take nail to the each of us brothers. We take each other by the hand. We take our hammers and nails and we hammer and nail all of these things, one by one at a time, we hammer all of these things into trees and into fencing posts, into backyard telephone poles and into the shingled sides of houses. But first, before we do the hammering in, we cover up all of these things with mud—this, to protect them, this, so that when somebody else comes into our town all that they see is mud. Us brothers, what we see, what we know, is everything that is under the mud: any thing and every thing in and of and from our dirty river town that might be up and picked up or taken away to some other place to be got rid of—some other place without all this mud and smoke and rust, a town, a world, without a muddy river running through it. And so, because of this, up against this, us brothers, we do what we can to stop this from happening. So this is what us brothers do. What we do is, we raise back our hammers. We line up those rusted nails.

The Moon is a Star

When the river dried to mud, us brothers, we walked down to the muddy banks of where the river used to be, and with our boy hands, digging down into this mud, us brothers, we dug down to where, we believed it, there was another river there, there was another river down beneath where our river used to be, there was another river there running underneath where this other river of ours was now just a river of mud. Us brothers, we dug down with our hands, we ate mud with our mouths, for three-hundred days and nights. For three-hundred days and three-hundred nights, us brothers, we dug and we dug until we dug ourselves down to where this mud, it turned back into river. Here in this under-the-river, under-the-mud river, this other river, underneath this mud, this river, it was even muddier here, here in this river, this river, it was even a dirtier river than the dirty river was that used to run its way through us brothers' dirty river town. There were no people down here, here in this other river world, down underneath where our dirty river used to be, there were no mothers or fathers to call us brothers Son, there were no other boys along this river to ask us to call them Brother too. There were no steel mills sitting shipwrecked on this river's muddied shore, there were no houses here built on or up from the river for us brothers to call our own, there was no town here for this dirty river to run its way through. No, there was only the river here, here by this other river underneath where our river used to be: there was only the mud of this other river holding this river in its place. There was no moon here, here by this other under-the-river river town with no town for this river to run its river through, there were no stars here in this other under-the-river world, there were no birds here, there were no fish here, no *singing* fish here, there was no Girl here for us brothers to say to her, Hey Girl. It was just us, the two of us brothers, with this river and the mud that this river made. It was just us and the three of us—brothers, river, mud—and for a while there was no other place for us brothers to want ourselves to be. But after a while, after a few hundred more nights of us brothers watching this other river flow on by our muddy boots' feet, us brothers, we said to each other, it was time now for us brothers not to be, all by ourselves, all alone with just each other and this river and mud. So, us brothers, what we did was, we dropped down, onto our hands and knees, down into the mud, and we started to make. We made, up from the mud, up from the river, we made Girl. We started at the bottom and made our way up. Girl's knees were especially muddy. Girl's knees, they were so beautiful, in their mudness, that us brothers, we wanted to stay forever on our knees kneeling. But then, so that we could better see Girl, here in this river night's dark, us brothers, we made us a moon for us brothers to better see Girl by. We made moon, out of mud, and we stuck it, this moon, up against the muddy night's sky. Girl took this moon, when she saw this moon, and she took a look inside it. Look inside it, Girl said to us brothers, and she lifted us up in her hands for us to see inside. Us brothers, we listened to, we did, what Girl said for us to do. We looked inside this moon. Inside this moon, there were girls, other than Girl, there inside this moon. Us brothers, we looked at these girls. Then, when we were done looking at these girls, we looked with our looks at each other. There was this look that us brothers, we sometimes liked to look at each other with this look. It was the kind of a look that actually hurt the eyes of the brother who was doing the looking. Imagine that look. Us brothers, looking with this look, we looked this look back away from each other. We looked with this look back into this made out of mud moon, into this moon with these girls there inside it. When we did this with this look, this moon, it shattered into a million pieces. Each broken piece became a star.

Which One of Us Brothers

Years later, when we are no longer boys, when we are brothers big and grown up to be brothers who are now men, we will sit down by the river's still-muddy banks, and one of us brothers big enough now to be called Mister will say to the other just as big brother: Girl always did like me best. We will the both of us brothers say that we were, by Girl, the best-liked brother between us. Us brothers, we will fight with our fists, we will duke it out, down by the river, to prove to each other, to prove to Girl, which one of us brothers was Girl's bestest brother, which one of us brothers Girl would have picked if she'd had to pick just one of us boys to do her girl things with. Picture the two of us grown-up-to-be-big brothers rolling around in the river's mud. See us walking out onto the river's water just so we can prove it to each other that walking out across the river's water can still be, by us brothers, done without us drowning. Imagine the moon, always big and full as it always was for us brothers, watching over the both of us: an eye, a lighthouse, a magnet, a hubcap, it is a skinned apple, it is a brother, it is a sister, to the both of us. But I was the brother, one of us brothers will say. No, I was the one. Us brothers, we will bat it back and forth like this, and this we will not stop, not until the stars fall burning from the sky: not until the sun refuses to rise and shine: not until Girl steps up out of the mud of the river to put an end to us brothers' fighting by saying, to the both of us brothers: I am large. I began as mud. I am of two mud hearts. I am big and I am girl enough for the both of you brothers. Here, brothers. And here Girl will hold out in her girl hands a heart in each hand that is a heart that is pumping away with mud. I am giving you both back your heart, Girl will say. To this, us brothers, we will both of us cry out, No, and No! On this, us brothers, we will both of us agree. We will see, us brothers, eye to eye. Okay, okay, Girl will say when she sees that this is so. Girl will hiss, Then quit all of this. Girl will insist that us brothers get along. Girl will make us brothers shake hands. Girl will go on to say, Go on now, brothers. Girl will nudge us brothers both a little closer. Kiss, Girl will tell us, and make mud. Girl will push us brothers out into the river. See the sky, Girl will say. Girl will force us brothers to let go of the moon's lit-up rope. Hold on to each other, Brothers. Girl will then push us brothers out from behind, out over the river's muddy edge. This, we will hear Girl whisper, into our ears. This is how you learn how to fly.

The Singing Fish: Revisited

This is how the story, the story of us brothers, this is how it ends. It ends as so many of our stories always do, at night, with us brothers running down to the dirty river that runs its way through this dirty river town. And so, this is how this story begins too: it begins with a river, and it ends with a river, and through it all there is the mud that holds this river in its place. So this is the river. This is us brothers. This is the story that is and will always be the both of us. It begins one night. One night, us brothers, we run ourselves down to the dirty river that runs its way through this dirty river town. Here, at the river's muddy shore, us brothers, because we are brothers, we drop down onto our hands and knees, down in the river-made mud, and down here on our hands and knees, down here where dirt and river kiss to make mud, us brothers, we bend down our heads, we close our boy eyes to the muddy darkness inside our own heads. Like this, us brothers, we take the muddy river's water into our mouths. We drink. We drink dirty river from dirty river, we breathe in buckets of rusty river water, we drink and we drink and we keep on with this drinking until there is no more river for us to drink. We drink, that is, until the muddy river turns into muddy mud. When it does, when the muddy river water turns to even muddier mud, like this, us brothers, picture us brothers, this will be the last you might ever see of us brothers: are you with us? Are you watching this? Are you down on your hands and knees drinking with us brothers? Now listen to us sing.

Fish Heads: Revisited

One day, us brothers, we get it into our boy heads to go with our hammers out back into the back of our yard, out back to where our fish-headed telephone pole is back there studded with the chopped off heads of fish. Back here we go with our hammers but not with our fists filled with rusty, bent-back nails, and here we start to unhammer and unnail, from this backyard pole, all of those fish heads that have been hammered and nailed into this telephone pole's wood. There are exactly one hundred and fifty fish heads hammered and nailed into that pole's creosoted wood, and so we take all one hundred and fifty of those fish heads down from where they have been hammered, and we put these fish, these fish heads, into our mud-rusty buckets and go—us brothers, we run with our buckets, one bucket hanging low off of each one of us brothers' arms, we go with these buckets filled up to their rims, we run ourselves down to the river, and one by one, fish head by fish head, we throw each one of these fishes' heads back into the river's muddy water. Fish, we say to these fish heads. Go back where you belong. Us brothers, we watch these fish heads float away and down the river, one by one they bob and they drift away on their way out to the lake, though when we get down to the last two fish, us brothers, we do not want to let these fishes go. We hold onto these last two fish, these last two of our fish heads, and we give each other this look. There is this look that us brothers, we like to look at each other with this look. This look, it's the kind of a look that actually hurts the face of the brother who is doing the looking. Imagine that look. It's while us brothers are looking at each other with this looking look that, out of the corners of each one of our eyes, the eyes of us brothers that are facing the river, us brothers, this is what we see: we see fish, we see fish heads, that have turned back into fish: fish with fish bodies and fish with fish fins and fish with fish tails to go along with their fish heads. These fish, they are swimming back upriver to where us brothers, we are standing, there on the river's muddy edge, and these fish, they are flopping themselves down into the mud that is muddy in and on and around our boot's feet. These fish, they are looking up at us brothers, up from this mud, with a fishy look on their fish faces that tells us brothers, Take us, brothers, home. Put us fishes back in our place. Nail us fishes back up and back into that back-of-the-yard pole. Us brothers, we give each other the look. We nod at each other with our boy heads. These fish, Brother says. These fish are keepers, Brother says. If you say so, I say to Brother. And then, fish by fish, brother by brother, us brothers, we fish our hands into our trouser pockets, we fish our knives up out of our pockets, we take each of us brothers turns cutting off, fish by fish, fish head by fish head, each of these fishes' heads.

And then, One Day, the Rains

And then, one day, the rains, the rains stopped raining down on our muddy river town, and all that mud that made our town the muddy river town that it was, all of that mud, it all dried up and turned to dirt. And the river, yes, the river, too, all of that muddy river water that made our muddy river the muddy river that it was, even the river and the mud that was at the bottom of the river, after not too long, it too turned to dirt. Yes, Brother, it was so dry in our dirty river town with a dirty river no longer running through it that when us brothers, when we walked down to where our muddy river used to be, what we found there instead of a river, there was just this dirt stretching out as far as our eyes could see. Water, no, there was no water anywhere that us brothers looked. And so, us brothers, what we did was, we walked out and across and out into the dirt hoping that where the dirt ended there would be water there and there would be the makings of mud there for us brothers to make into mud. And so we walked, and we walked, and we kept on walking on and on, across this dirt, walking with our faces pressing against the made-out-of-dirt sky. Us brothers, for four hundred days and four hundred more nights, we walked: in search of water, a river falling from the sky. A bird flying above us brothers would not have seen us brothers walking across dirt. All it would have seen was just dirt being blown across dirt. One morning, though, us brothers, we stopped our walking, and we found ourselves standing at the edge of a field of corn. This corn, it was growing up all brittled and stunted and brown up from all of this dirt. It was so dry, this corn, that when one of us brothers breathed, just the breath of us brothers breathing would make those corned stalks start to break. Or when we snapped off a shriveled-up ear and ripped off its papery husk, so dry were those skins that up from our hands they would blow and float away in a wind that was barely blowing. Inside, there were no yellow kernels to be found by us brothers: only the cobs themselves which would crumb apart and turn into dust. So what are we going to do? Brother was the one of us brothers brave enough to ask. I said to Brother that maybe it was time for us brothers to find something else for us to love: something other than river, other than fish. Something other than moon and girl and mud. But maybe I wasn't thinking is what I think now. Maybe there was so much dirt in my ears that I couldn't hear what it was that my mouth was saying. But we don't want to love something other than river and fish and mud was what Brother said to this. We love river, Brother said. We love fish. And mud, we can never get us enough of mud. I nodded my boy head at Brother. I know it, was what I said, and I shook my head so that my ears could better hear what my heart was wanting to say. You're right, Brother, I said, and I looked down at our dust-covered boots. I saw dirt there and everywhere underneath our feet. Dirt. I said this word, to myself, but I did not like the sound that this word made. I did not like the way that dirt felt in my mouth. It felt dirty on my tongue, this word dirt. Dirt was no good. The only thing dirt was good for was for turning dirt into mud. I did not have to say this to Brother. This, Brother already knew this. Us brothers, we looked across all of this dirt that was here in between us. We looked with this look that us brothers had between us. One look with this look and the both of us brothers knew that we did not need to make with our mouths another sound about this. And so, us brothers, us knowing this, we dropped down onto our hands and knees, down into this dirt, and like this, with our faces and fists pressed against the hardness that was this earth, us brothers, we began to hammer, we began to pound, we began to speak.

The Book of Mud

Tell us a story, us brothers said to Girl, the three of us sitting, down by the river, around the fire that the three of us had built. A story? Girl said. What kind of a story? A story about us, us brothers told her. But make it a story about us brothers that us brothers we don't know. Once upon a time there were two brothers, so began Girl's tale. But us brothers, we weren't the best listeners. Girl could not get beyond the first line before we started cutting in on her with questions, such as: what are their names? Where do they live? What is this story going to be about? To these questions, Girl came back with these answers: that these two brothers both called each other Brother, they lived near a river, and that mud is what their story was about. But we already know about that, us brothers said. To this, Girl didn't listen. Girl shook her girl head and then Girl started retelling her story. Once upon a time, she said, there were two brothers. And these brothers were brothers made out of mud. They were made out of mud and they didn't even know it. How do I know? Girl asked, and the fire flared up into our eyes. I know, Girl spoke this out, before us brothers could poke in our boy voices, because I was the one who made them. I was this girl, Girl said, who always wanted a brother, so I decided, one day, to make for myself not one brother but two. I started from the bottom and worked my way up. Only the moon above me, full and white, watched as I worked the mud up, mixing in river and dirt, until what stood up along side the river's edge on either side of my legs were these two made-out-of-mud brothers. The first words to come out of both of their mud mouths was the word mother. So that night, in a house not far from the river's muddy edge where these made-out-of-mud brothers got made, I found a woman who was not yet a mother and in her dream, that night, I whispered to her and told her that soon she was going to become a mother. When this mother awoke in the morning, she was sick and white-of-skin and inside her woman belly was a boat being rocked to and fro on stormy seas. The brothers were sailors on that sailoring ship sailing for a world that they did not know about. Months later, they came upon a muddy river that was more mud than it was water, and here they cast out their rusty anchors toward that muddy river shore. When they set foot onto all that mud, it was, to these brothers, like walking on water. They walked up from the river's muddy shore until they came upon the house where there lived this mother and a man too who these brothers would one day call father. Here these brothers lived and here they fished, and I watched without them seeing me, I watched them grow up, these brothers, into two muddy boys. And then one day I said to myself, it's time these boys know from where they came. So I came out of hiding. Under a moon big and full and white, I rose up out of the river's mud. Us brothers, when Girl said this, we leaned in even closer to this fire. This fire, it had grown bigger with each of Girl's breaths, each of her girl sentences was a log that Girl had pitched into the fire.

And now that Girl had stopped in the telling to us of this story, the fire was beginning to burn and fizzle out. Night swallowed us brothers up inside of its black-holed mouth. All the stars in the sky had fallen. The moon, it was a ghost of a fish blackened with mud. Us brothers, we got up and walked toward the river and then we kept on walking out into the dark and the muddy waters until the water was up and over our heads. In that underwater darkness below us brothers, with silver fish scales flashing in the spaces where the stars used to be, and with Girl's moony-eyed face gazing down at us from up above us brothers' head, we could hear the rivery gurgle of Girl's girl voice: And they lived, these brothers did. They lived happily ever after, Girl said. And here, us brothers, us looking up, looking up at the sky that was now the river, we could see Girl's hand closing in over the both of us—as if over a book—to hold us here in this place.

Good, Brother

When we fish the fish out of the dirty river that runs its way through this dirty river town: when we gut the fish: when we chop off the fishes' fishy heads: when we give each fish each a name: when we don't name the fishes Jimmy or John which is mine and my brother's name: when we take these fishes' chopped-off heads and then nail them, these heads, into the creosote-coated telephone pole out back in the back of our backyard: when our father calls out to us brothers: when he tells us that we are leaving this dirty river town: when our mother tells us too that we are going to be going, anywhere is the word she uses, just so long as anywhere is west of all of this mud and muddied water, away from all of this smoke and rust and steel: when to all of this all that us brothers can make our boy mouths say is but this is our house, but this is our river: when what our mother says to our buts is, we'll find us some other house for us to call our home, a place, she tells us once more, without so much mud and without those fishy river smells: when what we say to this is, but we love all this mud and the river and the fishy river smells is what we want our mother to know: when we look to our father, our father, we turn to him at times like these because we know that he, our father, loves mud too, that he, our father, loves fish too, that he, our father, loves the river too: when our father doesn't say anything to any of this: when our father just stands there not saying anything to any of this, not even those words but mother, or son, or boys, or fish: when, us brothers, to any and all of this, we don't know what we are going to do about it next: when that night, us brothers, sitting in our room, we look outside through our bedroom's window and see our fish, we see our fish-headed telephone pole, we see those fishes' chopped-off heads—open-eyed, open-mouthed—it's like they're singing out to us brothers what it is that we have to do next: when we go outside and walk down to the river and the river too, the river tells us what to do too: when the river and the fish heads both, they are one voice, a river of sound, running through the both of our boy heads, telling us brothers what we've got to do: when that night we go outside, out into the back of the backyard: when we go into our father's shed, where our father keeps his nuts and his bolts and screws, his buckets and ropes and ladders, and those bottles of his half filled up with whiskey: when we come back out and in our boy hands we are both of us brothers holding a hammer and a hand full of rusty, bent-back nails: when we walk ourselves and each other back to where our backyard telephone pole, it is all lit up and shining with the hammered in heads of fish: when I say to Brother, Brother, I say, you can go first: when I say to Brother, Brother, give me your hand: when Brother does like he is told: when I take Brother's hand into my own hand: when I hold Brother's hand up against this pole's creosoted wood: when I tell Brother, Brother, this might sting: when I reach back with my hammering hand: when I drive the rusty nail right through Brother's right hand:

when Brother doesn't even wince, or flinch with his body, or make with his boy mouth the sound of a brother crying out: when I say to Brother, Good, Brother: when I whisper this into his ear: when I raise back the hammer again: when I stop with the hammer: when our father, he steps out into the back of our backyard: when our father calls out to us brothers, Son: when, us brothers, we turn back away from each other, back toward the sound of our father: when we wait to hear whatever it is that our father wants us to do next: when we see that the sky down by the river, it is dark and quiet: when, us brothers, we know that, somewhere, the sun is shining: when what our father says to us then is, You boys be sure to wash up before you come back in: when us brothers, we nod with our heads, yes, yes: when we turn back to face back each other: when I raise back that hammer: when I look Brother in the eye: when I line up that rusted nail.